Ronald Reagan, My Father

Brian Joseph Davis

MISFIT

a misFit book

ECW Press

Published by ECW Press, 2120 Queen Street East, Suite 200,
Toronto, Ontario, Canada M4E 1E2
416.694.3348 / info@ecwpress.com

LIBRARY AND ARCHIVES CANADA CATALOGUING IN PUBLICATION

Davis, Brian Joseph, 1975-
Ronald Reagan, my father / Brian Joseph Davis.

ISBN 978-1-55022-917-2

I. Title.

PS8607.A953R65 2010   C813.6   C2009-905966-5

Editor for the press: Michael Holmes
Cover design: Shootthedesigner
Cover images: Library of Congress
Text: Rachel Ironstone
Printing: Friesens   1   2   3   4   5

Mixed Sources
Cert no. SW-COC-001271
© 1996 FSC
FSC

The publication of *Ronald Reagan, My Father* has been generously supported by the Canada
Council for the Arts, which last year invested $20.1 million in writing and publishing
throughout Canada, by the Ontario Arts Council, by the Government of Ontario through the
Ontario Book Publishing Tax Credit, by the OMDC Book Fund, an initiative of the Ontario
Media Development Corporation, and by the Government of Canada through the Book
Publishing Industry Development Program (BPIDP).

PRINTED AND BOUND IN CANADA

ECW PRESS
ecwpress.com

Biblical epigram removed by request of the rights holder

Contents

The Unicorns, Part One

Most days you would have already checked the cargo door with a weak tug, hit the light switch and watched the overhead fluorescents stutter out. You would have taken printouts of the day's last orders, put them on top of a black tray, grabbed your windbreaker, and left the light industrial park that you've worked in since you were a teenager.

But tonight, long after quitting time, you sat, digging your nails into your father's old oak desk. You were a print-on-demand publisher and you were being held hostage by the husband and wife team responsible for the 872-page *Index of Equine Characters in Fantasy Fiction*. It had not received a single order, and its authors were upset and armed.

The couple had similar features: competing jowls and oddly chopped curly hair that wanted to escape what it was attached to. At some point in his life the man had chosen to wear cargo shorts, a Joker T-shirt, and nothing else. The woman layered mismatched jogging apparel with a jean jacket covered in Bedazzler unicorns. Your business was designed so that you would never have to meet these people—a book is submitted, and for a fee it is laid out. Editing is extra. It gets stored on a computer until someone orders a copy. You inherited the business from your father. Well, not quite.

He started it as a song poem record company. Customers would send in their lyrics after finding an ad in the back of tabloids or music magazines that promised to *Set Your Poems To Music. Songwriters Make Thousands of Dollars. Free Evaluation.* Your father would perform the lyrics, no matter what they were, to either a thin pop waltz or a mild country stomp and send back a badly pressed 7-inch. Though at home he kept copies of the more ribald or peculiar ones— attempts at novelty songs about the Academy Awards streaker of 1974, or jingles about *Deep Throat*—and played them for friends doubled over in laughter after several Maker's Marks, your father taught you not to put yourself above the customer. "Be at least a little bit beside the customer," he said. "It helps."

You moved into the shop slowly, with your new ideas and photocopiers. As customers bought computers and realized their terrible desires in private, your father's orders shrank to a trickle. But you offered something different, a heftier object that was the end result of people buying computers, and the orders for books increased. Then one day, without telling him, you sold the 7-inch press and the lathe cutter to a small record company. The new owners—too young for their beards—high-fived after they loaded the greasy contraptions into a battered white van. Later, your father stared, confused, at the empty spot where the wall paint layers ended in the shape of the old machines. He stopped coming in.

It was your business now, and faceless senior citizen memoirists paid your lease. There were variations in routine. You once published a children's book titled *Mommy, Please Don't Wash Your Hands Again* by a housewife from Toledo. She had sent the order three times.

This man and woman were the first authors you had ever met, and you were surprised by how much they looked like the customers in your head, the ones you thought about as you reloaded toner into the photocopier on wan mornings. Your father was a musician, but you had never been a writer, and you felt you lacked an understanding of these people that he naturally had.

You tried to reason, hands waving in the air, that they had checked a web dialogue box, indicating they understood that you printed books and facilitated sales as a service publisher, but marketing was up to them. You wanted to be beside these people, but instead they were in front of you, ruining your tight-as-a-duck's-ass, wholly digital business with their three-dimensional realness.

When she took out a gun, you finally understood people: They will kill just to be heard, as easily as they will spend $39.95 to be published. You said, "Take whatever you want. Take my car keys."

The man asked you, "Have you ever written something? Have you ever actually written something?"

The woman screamed, "Call me Shadowfax!"

They demanded you perform for them. "Write something," he implored, as if you had forgotten what they were demanding.

"Call me Shadowfax," she said again, with a slight neigh.

You had often thought of stories while putting together shipments or sourcing new laser stock, but you never had the time to write them down.

Now, how much time you had left was dependent on how many stories you could write. Hands up and steady in the air, you asked if they wanted you to sit at the desk. She waved you over to your chair with the gun.

So you wrote and became, like them, strange.

Ordinary People

Pa never wanted to hurt people: neither before his execution, at the hands of the state of Texas, nor afterwards, when he came to be the focus of the only death penalty case that turned into a custody case that—my lawyer reckons—has turned into a right-to-die case.

The media tagged Pa as "the abnormal brain" in the whole "Reanimator of the Rio Grande" story, as it came to be known, but there was a man behind that brain. I know you expect a daughter to say so, but it was true.

Actually, there was a half-dozen men behind that brain—or, more specifically, parts of them. Back some time ago, Pa was arrested after his armed robbery of a Piggly Wiggly done went wronger than wrong can get. Two stockboys were shot and killed; their blood sprayed onto jars of pickled hotdogs, I was told.

Ma and me hadn't seen Pa in years at the time of the robbery. We heard he tweaked out on meth after getting laid off from a tool and die shop.

He was never the same after Vietnam, Ma recalled. Until he was drafted, he was as gentle as sweetgrass. After he shipped home and they hitched up, he started boozing and she booted him out not long after I came to be. It hurt her bad, she said many times, hand on heart, but she made the choice for my sake.

Pa went to trial—against the public defender's wishes—pleading the mitigating circumstances of his methamphetamine addiction. The judge rewarded Pa with the death penalty. When Ma and I said goodbye to him the morning of his execution he seemed more tired than anything. "Ain't this a heap a cowshit I rolled in?" he tossed over his shoulder as the warden ushered us out. Those were Pa's last words to me. His final last words to those gathered, truth be told, were "This government can suck my West Texas dick. Y'all hear that?"

That was his way with words. So you can see why Ma and I were surprised that Pa bequeathed his body to medical research. He figured there might be something to glean from looking at his tweaker's brain. "Probably look like an ol' dirty carburetor when those docs pull it out of my skull."

We mourned him and moved on, hearing nothing until, well, until you did. Seems that the university doctor who took Pa's brain away that night used it as the final touch for an experiment as audacious as it was unholy. This doc went and made himself a patchwork monster man that he then—through a process the doc took with him to the grave—got all alive and like. The investigators figured the doc jumped it with a car battery, given the electrodes on the head of the monster. Upon waking from eternal sleep, this monster destroyed the doctor's lab, ripped the arms off the doc, took those arms and continued to beat him with the arms. The monster—oh hell, let's just start calling him Pa—then rampaged through the campus till he was taken down in a hail of bullets after he stomped his way through a die-in of students protesting this current war.

Ronald Reagan, My Father

Pa—despite five hollow point shots—did not die for a second time. Guess 'cause the doc, sick sonobitch he was an' all, did do a bang up job. Give him that, I will.

Ma and I ran down to the hospital where Pa was chained up. He didn't speak much, just growled like a sick dog. But one of the nurses, a kind woman, discovered that the music of Charlie Daniels soothed this creature whose very existence replied "tough titty" to the laws of nature.

"It *is* Pa!" Ma and I cried in joy while looking in through the glass window. Though he had a different face—younger, like someone from a catalogue—Pa loved Charlie Daniels.

"No, it's Josh," a woman of about 30 or so said, walking up behind us and fighting for a look in through the window. "It's my husband's head. That's Josh."

The woman was Courtney Mellon-David, and clutching her side was her daughter Bethany—a bright and beautiful girl of five, no bigger than a thimble. And damn if this isn't where this whole cockeyed story gets as complicated as the game of cricket. Not a month before this, Courtney's husband died of a heart attack, and too young if you ask me. Josh Mellon-David was the lead project manager of a wildly successful web startup. Josh was a charitable man, we heard, who walked many miles for cancers he would never live to get. At work he was respected, but not feared by those below him. And he loved Bethany. No matter how busy he was at work, he would commute home for her ballet recitals or swimming lessons before driving back into downtown Dallas, where he would then lead his team through all night "imagineering" sessions.

Like my Pa, Josh willed all of his mortal remains to the embetterment of science. It was probably Josh's face—so JFK Jr.– like—that moved that doctor to saw off his head and make it the vessel of my tweaker Pa's dirty ol' carburetor.

"It's Josh and I can prove it." Courtney held up the smallest iPod you ever did see. "Josh loved Feist."

Courtney went into the room, smiling and taking small steps towards Pa, holding up the white ear buds in her shaking hands. She put the buds to Pa's mismatched ears, just below his electrodes. Pa frowned and made a mewling sound. He screamed something bloody and swatted at his head. He bit the iPod in half and strained at his chains, one of them popping out of its wall mount. Courtney was a smart girl—educated at Columbia we later found out. She stayed calm and was able to turn the Charlie Daniels CD back on. Pa stopped his rampage, whimpered, and swayed awkwardly to "Long Haired Country Boy."

Courtney came out of the room weeping, and Ma embraced her. Wished to say it stayed that cordial between us girls—two families now connected by this one act against nature. But it ended up back in the courts as we tried to figure out what took precedent in custody for the creature—the chicken, or the bucket the chicken resided in.

Actually, the first issue to be decided was whether the state of Texas was legally obligated to execute Pa again. We got hooked up, *for free*, with a sharp fellow from the Amnesty International. This lawyer proved that "as you cannot convict a man twice for the same offence, you may not execute him twice." Our lawyer also brought up—and this was risky considering our suit against Courtney—that there is possibly another life involved that could be affected. That of Josh's.

The judge threw his hands up, ultimately confounded by the philosophical entanglements. "Hell," the judge decided. "He is hereby released jointly to the families in shared custody until court hears arguments." That old judge brought down his gavel with a smirk that beamed *I quit,* and I don't blame him.

Ritalin helped Pa concentrate. Enough that he could move around town without shackles and do simple tasks. While waiting for the custody hearing we shared Pa-Josh, as we agreed to call him. Ma and I felt fancy and hyphenated, just like our new kin. Sometimes Courtney and Bethany would pick Pa-Josh up at our little place. Bethany took a while to warm up to him and had to be prodded by her mother. The papers made a lot out of Pa-Josh's fearsome countenance, lopsided arms, and too small head. But let me correct one thing: he did *not* smell of the grave. Pa-Josh was harvested from lab-quality cadavers only.

Sometimes we picked Pa-Josh up at the Mellon-David residence. While I didn't like to see Courtney swat smokes out of his mouth and admonish him, saying "Cigarettes. Bad. Fire. Bad," her home was such a beautiful place, with its real wood and two TVs and all, and those Gap clothes done made him look a lot more together. I felt something terrible bringing Pa-Josh back to our house, which, no matter how hard we tried, could never look so clean as the Mellon-David's.

Though a man could smoke a Pall Mall in peace here.

Well, it was while he was visiting his other family when this story got as complicated as the Electoral College vote. Pa-Josh escorted Bethany to her swimming lessons, and while the instructor was leading the other kids in leg-kicking exercises, Bethany floated off to the deep end, and the poor girl, she sank. Pa-Josh wasn't too bright since his operation—that's what we took to telling the neighbors— but he saw Bethany lying at the bottom of the deep end and did what needed to be done. He stepped into the pool and sank to the bottom, too. He picked Bethany up and started walking his slow shuffling walk up the slope to the shallow end. At the crest he collapsed.

Stupid thing forgot he couldn't breathe water. Bethany was revived by the lifeguard, but Pa-Josh, he never regained consciousness.

At the hospital, Courtney and I stood over him. He looked as forlorn as the end of a TV movie, what with those tubes doing his breathing. I looked towards Courtney and asked her, "Was Josh the kind of man who would want to be kept alive like this?"

"No."

"Neither was my Pa."

Courtney and I didn't discuss it. We just did it. Working quickly, turning machines off. Pa-Josh trembled and it was over. Well, over for Pa-Josh, rest his soul, or whatever car parts were in his chest.

Now Courtney and I are in court, again, this time as co-defendants.

Funny, you'd think those Christian folks would be happy to get rid of Pa-Josh, seeing as his existence kind of proved them all wrong. Nope. There they were, every day, outside the courthouse brayin' with signs a sayin' *A man designed his body badly, but God designed his soul intelligently* or *No separation of God and monsters!* They never had slogans for Pa the first time he done got pushed off this mortal sofa.

Ma's taking care of Bethany while Courtney and I are in the hoosegow so I guess we're kinda like a family now. Though I sometimes do think back upon Pa's final words to me.

No, not that guff about his West Texas dick. Rather, I think: *Ain't this a heap a cowshit I rolled in?*

Bury My Heart at Tataouine

Moussa sees the new visitors to his land with the perspective of countless millennia. The *Amenoka*—or chief—of a small population of Tuareg Berbers in southern Tunisia tells this reporter through translation: "We have wandered the desert from edge to edge since before time. We have protected our language and way. If they have come to the desert for their god, so be it. It will not upset us. We call them *kel Ataram* because they are from the West. They call us *Sand People*. We do not know why." His face covered by a deep indigo veil, he takes our crew to the site of the massacre that has shocked the international community.

Moussa is referring the growing population of *Star Wars* fans who have migrated to this arid region to live their life in monastic purity on the same land used for filming several of the franchise's most famous scenes. As a cattle herder and goods trader wandering the uppermost tip of the Sahara desert, Moussa has been witness to the birth of this new and little-seen sect. It's a group, it should be noted, not without its controversy here and at home. "They never wanted much in trade; I sold them two, perhaps three, DSL modems,"

Moussa says of the young people who called themselves the Rebel Alliance. "They wear brown robes. They are generally fat. Fat like boars and pale like milk. That is odd in the desert."

Odd, yes, but the group had odd beginnings. In the early 1990s, Lucasfilm Limited inaugurated the lucrative practice of guided tour packages to Tunisia. The company re-erected many of its sets as expensive hotels, which thrilled fans and became a steady revenue stream for creator George Lucas. Then in 2002, just after the release of *Star Wars: Episode II–Attack of the Clones*, a group of the fan tourists overtook their guides in the middle of a Wookie symposium and claimed the resort as their own state. Eyewitness accounts reported that the group celebrated for days and nights, playing what they called "Ewok music" on primitive drums and small Casio synthesizers.

The ringleader of the coup, calling himself Obi Wan Kevin, announced to an American diplomat soon after that the rebel sect wanted to return to the "true word" of Jedi Masters and to "purge the franchise of control by the dark side." Though born Kevin Oakley in Ann Arbor, Michigan, to liberal school teacher parents—and known as "The Oak" to high school peers because of his girth—Oakley quickly ascended the ranks of Star Wars fandom to control the most popular web site dedicated to the series, *The Dagobah Times*. A key theologist in the "Jedihadist" school of fandom, Oakley made his first headlines only a month before the coup when he issued an Internet-wide *fatwa*, calling for the head of actor Hayden Christensen, the wooden thespian who was given the role of a young Anakin Skywalker. The FBI was preparing an indictment against Oakley for the death threats when he disappeared. He did not surface until the events in Tunisia.

Some members of the group trickled back to various embassies only days into the siege, telling horror stories of Obi Wan

Kevin's dictatorial methods. Neophytes were often beaten while blindfolded, with Obi Wan Kevin admonishing them to "Use the force. Use the force." Now most Americans know Obi Wan Kevin from video footage of the bearded, dirty, and wild-eyed messiah on a stretcher after capture. He has since been incarcerated for five years without trial. The U.S. Army has blocked all efforts by the press and the Oakley family to contact him. It has been rumored that the capture of Obi Wan Kevin was made possible by tips from his own lieutenants.

Yet the colony Obi Wan Kevin founded thrived, and members accepted the fate of their captured leader as "just like being frozen in carbonite." Lucasfilm has officially washed its hands of its properties in the area, denying any responsibilty for the city now christened "New Alderaan." Attempts to confirm this story with the Tunisian government were also met with silence. Tunisia is tight-lipped about its affairs in general, and the region in question is little populated, save for the Berbers and the newcomers. Until two weeks ago, initiates were arriving daily, resulting in an estimated colony of 500.

"Most have scattered to the mountains," Moussa says as we near what the sect called the Cantina. "They will talk to us, but no one else." It was Moussa who discovered last month's carnage. As he closed upon the small settlement with his herd in tow, he saw something wrong. "Many times when I passed at dawn, they played with sticks, either blue or red in color, hitting each other. That day I saw buzzards. Going closer there were many bodies."

Those bodies are now gone, removed by the Red Cross, but the "sticks" lay on ground, already being covered by the gusting sand.

Knowing the Cantina building to be a mosque originally, our producer asks Moussa if he thinks religion may have been behind the attacks. "No," he answers. Moussa then takes from under his coat a wine bottle. Passing it to our cameraman, Moussa says, "Look not towards Mecca, but west, to Napa."

Moussa and others claim to have found several drained bottles of 2002 Skywalker Ranch *Viandante del Cielo Chardonnay* around the massacre site. These bottles fueled rumors that Lucasfilm was holding a summit with the sect, one that ended with misunderstanding and bloodshed. While this theory was posted on Metafilter by a user with the screen name "Yoda's Choda," the State Department is taking it seriously enough to investigate the movements of several Lucasfilm executives in the last month.

Yet with sect members still in hiding, and given the vastness of the desert itself, a full picture of what happened at New Alderaan is not likely anytime soon.

Without anyone tending to the buildings, the sand is already climbing the sides of the whitewashed domes and creeping into open doorways. The immense riches of *Star Wars* collectibles that fill nearly every corner of every structure are slowly warping and fusing into one plastic mass in the heat. I pick an oversized Boba Fett figure up off the floor. Once valued for its see-through scope eye, smaller figurines are stuck to the doll like clusters of coral.

Next week, Moussa will be leaving the area and taking his herd north as summer hits the desert and the already oven-like temperatures increase. "One must move with the sand. That is what the desert asks of us."

The Gift of the Twelfth Congressional District of Michigan

1.

Paul parked his Gremlin in the strip mall lot as night settled in. He hefted his body out of the car, feeling like his belly dragged behind a few good seconds. Approaching the door of his small law office he peered through the glass, past taped-on posters in red, white, and blue that urged citizens to "Vote Paul Poplawski for Congress," and his personal least favorite, "Pops is the tops for the House!" That one was Mitch's idea. No one had ever called Paul "Pops" before.

His two volunteer phone girls were gone, but Mitch, his campaign manager, was still at his desk. Paul ambled in, glanced at a pile of mail and noticed a coupon sheet for Little Caesars. Mitch was lost in large printouts blanketing the desk—probably more columns of voter demographics and statistics that confused the hell out of Paul and cost him too much money. He pocketed the Little Caesars coupon. "Mitch, what are you still doing here?" he asked.

Not looking up, Mitch replied, "Trying to get you elected, last time I checked. And driving a car not made in Detroit still isn't helping. I told you to borrow your brother's T-bird."

Paul had steered his campaign haphazardly and he knew he would likely not win. He saw it through because he believed that it was every American's right to run a faltering, under-funded campaign. But hiring Mitch, a fresh graduate in something called Communications, got Paul closer than he thought he could to Congress. "Just stop— stop your calculations for one second," Paul stammered. "Your dad, Mitch? You should be at the funeral home. Making arrangements."

Mitch hoisted up his pale moon face and took off his glasses, which had the effect of making his button eyes disappear into even smaller dots. It struck Paul that Mitch was as ugly as his printouts.

"The Twelfth District is 30 percent UAW," Mitch declared. "But we can get them. They are mad as hell at Carter over this hostage thing."

"Listen to me. I don't care how long ago your dad left, he's your dad. You will regret not being part of this."

"We run an ad on values. At the same time we do a final phone survey of UAW members where we ask, 'Would you feel the same way about your candidate if you knew that he was arrested at a swingers' party?' Image and values are how we're going to win this thing. One ad. Twenty phone workers. That's all we need."

"There's no more money left, Mitch. Get your coat on. I'll drive you there." As an afterthought, Paul added, "In my car not made in Detroit."

Mitch looked down again, past his printouts, towards the ash-colored carpet. He was the same color.

Paul thumbed the coupons and took them reluctantly out of his pocket, tearing off a corner and handing it to Mitch. "Go next door, get some food for god's sake. You look terrible."

2.

In the previous months of campaign work Mitch had grown to hate Paul, though the low rent candidate was tolerated for the sole reason that he could, in spite of himself, win. So Mitch focused on the candidates—senatorial, gubernatorial—who would hire him after he installed Paul as a one-term oddity who cruised in on the rancor vote. The party had already noticed Mitch's fine, if frustrated, work with Paul. Mitch told him to trim his sideburns and button his collar, but Paul would just buy louder shirts and look more and more like the son of a Hamtramck butcher. The candidate's refusal to finish the fight during the final weeks was a willful acknowledgement that losing was possible.

Mitch scuttled down to the corner of the strip mall where Little Caesars glowed orange. As he grabbed the door handle he looked across the lot and saw his father's car idling, the exhaust filling the air with compact clouds. He was shocked for a second before figuring it out.

"Damn," he muttered to himself. "Not now, Donald."

Inside, Mitch ordered his food and then sat at a stool by the window. It would be his first time eating since being told his father had died the night before of a heart attack. That morning his mother sent word that she wouldn't be able to fly in from Montana in time. She told him whatever he and Donald decided would be best.

His father had left the family slowly enough that most people barely noticed. As a geologist for Shell Oil, he traveled for weeks at a time, and at home he was a tall, sullen shadow. When Mitch was eight, the weeks that his father was away had turned into months. His mother sat him down and told him that his father would be living with someone else. A friend named Donald.

As Mitch grew older, his father grew tanner, and more expressive, than a sullen shadow. The happiness put weight on his face, a kind of vague chubbiness Mitch was just now inheriting. And then came the sound. At first it was a single chime in time with his father's steps as he walked out the door to greet Mitch at the start of a visitation weekend. After several years, the sound became like carillon bells, tolling every step he made.

In '68, his father planned a Disneyland vacation with Mitch. They made it to the airport gate where they stood in line and wondered what was taking so long. When a woman in an airline vest and beehive passed by, Mitch's father tapped her arm and asked what the heck that contraption was up ahead. The woman explained it was a metal detector and that "Yes, it's totally harmless." She walked on, and after several seconds, Mitch's father crouched down. "We're having a family emergency. I'm sorry." With that they left the airport.

The door to Little Caesars opened and fresh cold air collided with the smell of pizza. A man with close-cropped peppered hair and a still-dark mustache walked in.

"Donald," Mitch whisper-shouted at him. "I said we'd figure things out later."

"I'm sorry, Mitchell. Your mom told me where you were. I just had a panic. First he's at the hospital and I couldn't see him, and now he's dead, and he's going to the funeral home, and I just—I just need your help."

"Okay, sit down, Donald. You know I will go along with whatever you want."

Donald eased onto a stool next to Mitch. "I know they're going to steal it all."

"Steal what?"

"His gold."

"His what?"

Donald glanced around and leaned in, "His jewelry."

It was during a break from college that Mitch finally learned where the chiming came from. At a Tigers game he and his father went into the restroom. As usual, he went to a stall and Mitch went to the trough. The stall that day amplified his father's miraculous chiming sound, much like a belfry. Other men looked up and, rather than feeling pleasantly surprised at the sudden sound of ethereal metal crickets in their presence, left the restroom after hastily finishing their silent shaking. Mitch joined them, feeling like a coward for being afraid of his father's musicality. When his father came out of the stall, the room was empty.

At his father's house the next morning, Mitch found a magazine on the kitchen table. Crudely printed, it featured black-and-white photographs of men and women displaying painful-looking but elegant rings and studs on their bodies and through flaps of skin. Mitch opened the magazine to a centerfold. It was a close-up of a flaccid penis adorned with religious care, studded with metal bumps and loops. The poser was kneeling on a Hudson's Bay blanket that Mitch remembered from the guest room. The spread was at once as otherworldly as a page of *National Geographic* and as hokey and suburban as a church bulletin. The caption read, "'Dr. Rock' is a scientist who holds on to our record with his 41st piercing!" Mitch felt familial honor despite his confusion. His father was always the winning type.

"He was so afraid of metal detectors at the airport," Donald said. "That's why he started using solid gold. I know you don't want to hear about it, but it *was* him and it *was* everything he had."

Mitch figured he could get several thousand dollars for his father's jewelry. For much of 1980, gold had been selling at $900 an ounce.

This was one thing to thank Carter for, Mitch thought. There would be more than enough for some real phone workers and an ad that could even run on Channel 7 instead of Channel 50. He would just tell Paul that the donor wanted to remain anonymous.

"Okay, Donald. I have a meeting with the campaign staff right now. Tomorrow, you'll come to the funeral home with me. For now, go home, phone some friends. I'll see you in the morning."

They stood up and Donald hugged Mitch, who received the embrace with back slaps.

"Your dad never forgave himself for not being around to see you grow up, you know that?" Donald asked as Mitch went to the counter for his Crazy Bread.

3.

As Paul drove them to the Stavro Funeral Home, Mitch forced himself to eat the fast food. Mr. Stavro, who let them in, was a man with slicked down white hair and a matching carnation in the lapel of his brown suede suit. Paul sat in the lobby as Mr. Stavro and Mitch moved into an office.

"Your father is now here," Mr. Stavro explained as he and Mitch walked. "No checks tonight. We worry later. We just need to set the times for the visitation and services."

"What I'm wondering is if I could spend some time alone with my father? A few minutes."

"Oh, we do not recommend it," Mr. Stavro said with a shaking index finger. "We do much to present the deceased in a certain manner, and your father, he has just come from the hospital."

"I didn't get a chance to say goodbye."

It was a line Mitch plucked from some TV-imbedded memory, and it did not seem to work.

"Our licences do not permit." Stavro shuffled a stack of prayer cards.

Mitch took a crumpled $20 bill out of his front pocket. Mr. Stavro nodded his head.

He led Mitch to the chapel and through a door at the back into a hallway that had the unkempt feel of backstage. Around a corner they came to a cinderblock room, half garage and half lab. On a gurney a body lay covered in a winding sheet.

"We leave you now," Mr. Stavro finished, with a slight bow.

With short steps Mitch walked to the body. He reached his hand out and saw it trembling. His father lived the life he wanted to live and the onus to do the same would be Mitch's inheritance. With the courage of that thought, he pulled back the bottom half of the sheet, leaving the face covered.

His father's shirt was left torn open, probably from when the paramedics treated him. The violation angered Mitch, who noticed a lightening bolt–shaped burn on the stomach, leading down to below his father's belt. What Mitch had come to steal had acted as a conductor when they put the paddles on him.

Mitch undid his father's belt and pants. He tugged the polyester open and down as much as could. As the body jostled, the jewelry made its chiming sound and when Mitch heard it, he wept. He edged the pants down more and more until he saw the gold. His father's crotch seemed made of gold and Mitch didn't have a clue how to remove any of it.

Some were like hoop earrings and he snapped them open, quickly putting them in his pocket. The golden ribs that dotted the shaft turned out to be barbell shaped doohickeys with ends that unscrewed. This took time, and Mitch abandoned his harvesting after only 10 of them. He continued weeping and sniffling as he plucked off diamond shaped plumbs—four of them—that dangled from chains. He did calculations as to how much airtime each piece of gold would purchase, but halted at the horseshoe-shaped piece. It was the largest, and its placement through the head and out the urethra filled Mitch with terror and wonder at the depth of his father's experiences and how he had found more mystery in his life than a geologist for Shell Oil had the right to find. Mitch tugged at the horseshoe but with the body's rigor mortis well set in, the golden thing would not budge. Mitch tugged and wept.

4.

While waiting in the lobby, Paul had settled on purchasing the ad time and hiring the extra help. To say no was to say no to Mitch, who ran this campaign as if he himself would be heading to Washington, working even on the day his father died. What was the cost? Paul thought. It was a couple of payments on the boat, and he hadn't even been out on Lake St. Clair once the previous summer.

He was fully taken over by the delirium of boat payment math when Mr. Stavro came and suggested that the bereaved seemed to be upset and that perhaps it was time to collect him.

Mr. Stavro pointed Paul towards the cinder block room and, as Paul found his way, he heard Mitch's sobs echoing down the hall. "Pops" Mr. Stavro announced before leaving, "You have our vote."

Paul wanted nothing more than to go to Mitch, put a hand on his shoulder and tell him tears were okay, that fathers disappeared. That's what they did, every morning while we grow up, and then permanently.

But Paul never had the chance to begin his homily. As he entered the room the whiteness reminded him of the butcher shop of his childhood, how it was clean and horrifying. Mitch's back was to Paul, hunched and lurching with sobs that sounded like snores flapping through jowls. Before Paul could open his mouth he saw Mitch's arm moving up and down, pushing around the body's groin area. Up and down, up and down—Paul's eyes followed in shock. But his ears were lulled by the gentle chiming sound that filled the room.

Paul understood that grief could drive men to strange acts, but even with all his knowledge gleaned from 20 years in real estate law, he didn't have a damn clue about what was going on in front of him.

He edged out of the room. Paul would return to the lobby, he resolved. He would sit down and wait for his campaign manager, telling Mr. Stavro that everything was all right. Paul would speak as little as possible on the ride to Mitch's apartment. Paul would say good night and, with respect for the dead in mind, wait until tomorrow to fire Mitch, who in the end was right. Politics did come down to image and values. Pops had to stay tops.

The Libertine

1.

Clive awoke to the sound of an automobile crashing outside his cottage. "Bollocks," he complained in disbelief. Feeling the empty side of his bed he remembered his wife was not there. Candace and the children left that morning to visit her sister in Bromley. Wearing only trousers and an undershirt, Clive went outside into the early Wolvercote morning. He could see his breath. The crash had long echoed out and left behind a single car—a small blue Peugeot rolled on its side near a copse of trees—and the sound of a woman crying. Clive increased his gait. Putting a slippered foot onto the drive shaft he hoisted himself up and looked into the cab. "Jenny?" he asked the woman wiggling herself out of the passenger seat.

Below her was the dead body of Mayor McCheese.

Clive grabbed Jenny's arm through the window. Pulling herself up, she stepped obliviously onto Mayor McCheese's face, her pump heel crushing his soft yellow bun skull and those layered hamburger patties that formed his mouth. Clive helped Jenny onto the ground and then looked back in at the soup. "Bloody hell," he hissed. Floating in the puddle of condiments and bun crumbs was a half-empty bottle of vodka. Clive lowered himself in and, legs braced against the sides, reached down to pluck out the ketchup- and mustard-covered bottle with a sucking sound.

He went to where Jenny sat on the ground. "Okay, old girl," he said. "Let's go." He hurried her back to the cottage and led her inside and upstairs to the bedroom. As Clive laid her on the bed he looked down and noticed shoe-shaped smears of condiments on the carpet.

"I'm sorry," Jenny slurred. "We thought you were gone to London. You always were."

He remembered the bottle in his hand, then went downstairs to find a bin liner in which to stow it away. There was a knock on the door. Clive dropped the bottle to the ground where it broke. Kicking the glass aside, he washed his hands quickly while the knocking continued. Clive answered the door.

"Sorry to disturb you, Professor," the constable offered with a tip of his hat, "But there's an accident down the way and I thought you—"

"I was sleeping until you knocked."

"Your lights were on that's all."

"Are they hurt?"

"Dead. Just one. Just one fellow there is. A Yank as far as we can tell."

"How can you tell?"

"He got a hamburger patty for a noggin, he does. 'Avin a late night snack, Professor?"

"No. Why do you ask?"

"Spot o' mustard on your trousers. Right there."

2.

Clive walked into the kitchen and set his lecture notes and papers down onto the table. Candace was washing up dishes. He snuck up and embraced her. "Never mind, you," she lightly scolded, playfully batting him away with suds. "I am trying to wash up last night's supper plates that you forgot about."

"I invited some grad students over for lunch tomorrow. And Mayor McCheese. You know that bloke visiting from the States? The one who's promoting those new restaurants here?"

Candace stared hard back at Clive.

"All right. A cold lunch then, luv. And don't worry about McCheese. I've already spoke with him regarding those blue jokes."

"Is Jenny coming?"

"Yes, with Peter."

"She's lovely, isn't she? Reminds me of Deborah Kerr."

"She's bringing Peter down, if you ask me."

The next day Jenny and Peter arrived. Mayor McCheese was late. Candace set food out and left the trio to discuss department gossip in the backyard as she went to nap with the children. "You know, I might take a break from the degree," Peter said, looking towards the nearby canal, swirling the melting ice around in his gimlet.

In a slight stupor of heat and gin Clive attempted comment, but Mayor McCheese arrived and conversation came alive, turning to talk of adverts, franchises, and the mayor's friendship with Steve McQueen. Despite the excitement over the foreigner, Peter kept turning the conversation back to Clive, finally asking for a walk.

"All right then, sport," Clive told Peter gamely. "Off we go."

As they walked down to the canal Peter glanced back at the American and Jenny. Mayor McCheese seemed to be telling a funny story, his gloved hands and tiny top hat waving in the air. "Clive, I'm going to do it."

"Do what?" Clive replied, still looking at Jenny. "Leave school?"

"No. Ask Jenny to marry me. I'm afraid what I said before about leaving school was a bit of a ruse. But what do you think? She and I have been living together rather well."

"Well?"

"I am asking you what you think."

"I think a break from school is healthy thing. For someone like you."

Hand in hand, Jenny and Mayor McCheese ran towards the men. "Peter," Jenny blurted out. "Our mayor has the most delightful story about Liza Minnelli. You simply must hear it. And you have been hogging our lecturer of Restoration comedy." Jenny took Clive's elbow crook and walked him away from Mayor McCheese and Peter.

Clive looked down and caught a glimpse of a light blue bra strap escaping from under her blouse. She pulled it back then asked, "He's a laff, innit he?"

"Peter?"

"No," she shouted out while tapping Clive on the chest. She coyly lowered her voice. "Mayor McCheese."

"There already is a Mrs. McCheese."

"Really?" Jenny faked badly. "Do you know the Mayor said I'd be perfect for an advert they're filming in a few weeks?"

"How would I know he asked you? He just told you."

"Always the headmaster, eh? It's just for a laff, Clive. And Pinter is directing."

"Then do it."

Peter and Mayor McCheese merged back with Clive and Jenny along the canal. "Oi!" Peter cried out. "Let's play Yahtzee."

3.

Near the end of the day of the advert shoot Clive drove to the studio and waited in the parking lot. Jenny didn't show. After a half hour he looked at his watch, then got out, slammed the door, and skulked into the studio where the stage was already shutting down. There were foam trees, a smiling felt sun, and a field of baby hamburger puppets being gathered off the fake farm set. *So this is McDonaldland*, he thought.

Clive found a technician coiling wire and asked if Jenny was still around. A different man, pushing a camera out of the way shouted, "Try the office upstairs. She's getting 'er next job she is." Several old workers exploded with toothless giggles. Embarrassed, Clive left and sat in his car. Jenny dashed out sometime later.

She hopped in.

"Thanks for the lift back," she said, pecking Clive's cheek. He caught a whiff of pickle and winced.

"Do you get overtime?"

"Are you jealous, Clive? How adorable. Mayor McCheese loves to talk and that's all. You know those Americans."

Clive drove out of the city. Dusk turned into night before he asked her, "How long have you've been seeing him?"

"Since we met."

"That night?" Clive shouted out. "At my house? With Peter there?"

"I don't believe you. You don't like Peter anymore than I do. Mayor McCheese is different. I want different."

"You've got cheese in your hair."

"Don't judge me like that, Clive. Not you."

Smokestacks and trees blurred by. "He's really Scottish then, is he?" Clive deadpanned.

They both laughed.

Two blocks from her and Peter's flat, Clive pulled the car over near a streetlamp. "We're going to the city over the next few weekends, Candace and I," he mumbled, not looking at Jenny. "Her sister is pregnant again. You remember where the key is, right?"

"You know, he says he has friends at Yaddo."

4.

Clive shut the door on the constable. While he appeared satisfied with Clive's answers the constable seemed to be stretching his gaze past him. Clive now looked around his own home suspiciously; how quickly it became a mess in the 15 hours without Candace. He had feigned a fever and stayed back for the weekend. Candace obliged his performance, even refusing his unshaven peck at the doorway as she and the children left.

He waited for Jenny and their American friend, drinking wine throughout the bright day. By 8 p.m. he was too drunk to get up off the divan and ended up urinating into the empty wine bottle. Jenny and Mayor McCheese never arrived. Somehow Clive ambled to bed, set the full, warm wine bottle on the nightstand, and passed out.

"You were driving the car, weren't you?" Clive asked as he ran back in the bedroom where Jenny now lay sobbing.

"No."

Clive threw himself onto Jenny, pinned her arms down and held his face close to hers. "Tell the fucking truth. You were driving. You were driving, weren't you?"

"No!" Jenny screamed, writhing under his weight. Clive backed off and sat on the edge of his bed. "Yes," Jenny shrieked, rolling over into the pillow. "Yes, I bloody fucking well was driving."

He stood up and went to the window. Down the way, an old lorry's lights were flashing, ready to take the ruined car and dead man away. Clive didn't know if, when they righted that car, they'd find a purse or a bracelet. This was still the countryside, and uncomfortable questions were often left respectably unanswered, even for Americans with a hamburger patty for a noggin.

"Fond of him?" Clive asked, still looking out the window.

"You?" Jenny spat back.

Clive held his hand flat against the window, leaving marks. He took his hand away, thinking that Candace would only have to clean up after him.

5.

Clive had followed Jenny and Mayor McCheese to Soho one morning, staying several automobiles behind the blue Peugeot, feeling much more like Michael Caine than a lecturer on Restoration comedy. Jenny and the American parked in an impossibly narrow cobblestone alley and darted around a corner. Clive waited several breaths and followed them to a door under the burned out marquee of *Continental Cinema Arts*. Entering into a lobby staffed by a lone geezer, Clive paid the one-pound admission to *Belgian Spa*, now in its third hit week according to a sign etched in blue Biro.

The cinema sat 50, at most, and there were only a few punters spread around. Clive perched at the back and saw Mayor McCheese's oblong head silhouetted by scratched, sputtering flesh blurs on the screen. It was then that the mayor's head struck Clive as a spaceship of some kind. Jenny, beside the mayor, rubbed closer to the spaceship, her arm and shoulder slowly falling down and up—a handjob, as the Yanks called it. Clive had heard his students talk about them and often thought it sound like a service to be checked off on a contractor's estimate.

As the film and Jenny's arm continued their cyclical movements, Clive noticed the punters, seemingly out of feral instinct, start to move closer to the couple, seat by seat. Clive got up, hopping one aisle, then another. He wanted to warn Jenny about the perverts, about where she was. Clive felt the projection light catch his face. He sat down quickly, slunking into his new seat. Clive beat all the other punters and was alone at the end of Jenny and Mayor McCheese's aisle, looking at them, looking at the screen, looking at Jenny's hand, and then looking at his own.

The Bourguignon Prize

Me good poet.
Me brain damaged.
No one notice.
Not always like this.
Thoughts hurt head.
Doctor say thing more clear.

"Patient Laurie Beal, aged 38, presented on July 6 with severe headaches, high fever, photophobia, and intermittent confusion. A preliminary diagnosis of encephalitis was made and the patient admitted. Patient history revealed that a month previous she held a backyard party at dusk and, in a rush to make a complicated hummus recipe, forewent the purchasing of citronella candles despite warnings of West Nile–infected mosquitoes in her area. The next day she experienced headaches and malaise but believed it to be eyestrain from her job as copy editor at an alternative weekly, or stress regarding a recent volume of poetry she published that had gone unnoticed. This gave way to joint pain and rash and finally fever and headaches. The etiology was consistent with West Nile encephalitis and treatment was begun while CSF test was performed to confirm infection."

Me write first poetry book once.
Trade critic write
only review.

"Beal may be a talented poet one day but for now she is too in love with her own cleverness. Her long, trill lines contain references within references and allusions to allusions. Baroque and embellished with rich, polysaturated words, Beal has made a feast that attempts too much and rewards too little our passing interest."

Doctor say,
no more poem.
Words missing
in my brain.

"MRI revealed severe encephalitis with limbic involvement. CSF confirmed West Nile infection and symptomatic treatment maintained. Fever continued to spike and patient lapsed into a two-day coma. She remained stable but febrile and damage could not be ascertained until she was revived."

Me angry now,
all time.
Light invade head.
Words now
hurt like

something breaking
in head.

"Cognitive testing revealed severe limbic system damage. Emotions were uncontrollable, with a violent fascination with ears. Patient attacked several physicians and nurses. Patient given Clozapine to quell psychotic episodes. While memory was not impaired, patient's verbal and written communication was truncated and severely debilitated, with lack of metaphor and simile construction. Given her uncontrollable outbursts, patient should be treated under restraint and secure supervision. Prognosis for full recovery: 10%. Prognosis for partial recovery: 40%."

Me escape hospital.
Me show teeth at nurse.
They run.
Me no longer poet.
Me monster.
Me just copy editor.
Me go work.
Me sit down,
hit keyboard,
make words good.
No one notice,
me talk no good.
Wear gown.
Under clothes.
Drooling.
Me have
newfound talent

for sidebar,
they say.
Me still want
eat ear.
Must not eat ear.
Magazine industry
not working.
Many pack boxes.
Hug from no-longer-editor.
Rip ear,
from his head.
Chew.
Police.
Hospital.
Gawker.

"BLIND ITEM: During a round of layoffs at an august alt-weekly, a copy editor turned cannibal and chewed off a recently fired editor's ear. See, you gotta watch those spaces before and after the em dashes, or else!

UPDATE: Turns out the copy-editing cannibal is also a poet. Check out her poems after the jump."

Me write poems
in hospital.
Look like this.
Me take pills.
Stop ear eating.
Kinda.
Poetry is

practice words.
Send poems to
publisher.
Publisher e-mail words.
Words hurt head.
Me want eat
her ears.

"Laurie, I'd like to say how speechless I am regarding your new work. These poems hum with the essence of life. While I absolutely adore your previous works, with their long, ornate sentences, these are a breakthrough in linguistic simplicity and emotional fire. Oh, and 'ear eating': my God, what a powerful metaphor for the information age."

Me publish second book.
Too many person
like.
Trade critic think
it good.
Me think they think
brain damage good.

"Laurie Beal is the poet of the Twitter age. She has wildly abandoned all unnecessary language and in doing so forces us to focus only on that which is painfully real. Throughout she returns to a central image of ear eating. It's ghastly and violent but also a warning from the poet about the limited power of words and how we all fail to communicate."

Words no limited.
Me is.

"There is a great mind at work here."

Me get money.
Doris L. Kohl Award for Poetic Excellence,
The Transportation Secretary's Award for Poetry,
The Lucky-You Second Book of Poetry Award.
Me want eat
Doris L. Kohl
ear of excellence!
Publisher submit me
to fellowship grant.
Two-year research.
What me want research?
Me research ear eat!
Me get ear eat grant.
Me get more nomination.
The Bourguignon Prize.
100,000 money.
Me taken to gala.
Me forget pills.
Me introduced.

"No poet has developed such a rich language as has Beal. Her spaces are mysteries. Half-opened doors that she beckons us to walk through. Her bravery becomes ours and we walk through. On the other side is a battlefield where our sense organs, like our ears, are the victims. The poet has given us a metaphor for life in wartime."

Words hurt head.
Poet me goes to
toilet.
Look for pills.
Woman comes in.
Other poet. Not me.
Hate me.
She smiles.
Ears move!
More smile.
More move ears.
Ritz Bitz
ears.
Adjectives have returned!
Partial recovery.
But ears
still
move
to
my
mouth.
Drool.
Then me,
hear big echo,

"And the Bourguignon Prize is awarded to Laurie Beal."

Other poet takes my small hand.
We leave the white washroom.
Walk to tall stage.

Think of what to
spend green money on.
West Nile.
Lots of West Nile.
In big blood supply.
In small animals.
In small, small, mosquitoes.
Make big brain,
in small you.
Make my
epiphany
yours too.
Me good poet,
like that.

Johnny

1.

"Let me tell you about Johnny, daddy-o. If I were you I wouldn't mess around with Johnny. He don't like nobody on his back. Johnny's got his own demons. You wanna see something? You wanna see Johnny go? He can really go. He can really screw it on. Johnny says we gotta hang around and wait. Johnny insisted on meeting you. Don't you think you should be interested in Johnny's payments to me. I think you should be. You seen Johnny Boy tonight? I don't know where Johnny is, what trouble he got into. I don't know if you'll find him right away. He probably heard about the trouble today. Johnny's a pretty smart guy. If Johnny is late again, I hope he can dance with a broken leg. I always know where to find Johnny. In the casino losing his shirt. That Johnny. He'll be the death of me. He's one in a million, that Johnny. If you're worried about Johnny, don't be. I hate him. That's how it's been ever since Johnny and his cowboys took over the local.

"Ah, the good old days, before Johnny went AWOL. You can't take it so seriously. After all, it's Johnny. Johnny's right for this ranch. He's no hothead. I know I can count on Johnny to continue my work. Johnny does you favors, kid. You got to do a little one for him once in a while. Let's do it for Johnny. We'll do it for Johnny! Isn't Johnny terrible? He's simply too fantastic for words. Oh, I've got all the faith in the world in Johnny. Whatever he does is all right with me. If he wants to dream for a while, he can dream for a while, and if he wants to come back and sell peanuts, oh how I'll believe in those peanuts! And then we can spend the money for Johnny's surgery.

"Well, does anybody really know Johnny? I don't think that Johnny likes me. Johnny is such a hard name to remember and so easy to forget. All I really want is for Johnny to love me like he did in high school. I was crazy about wanting Johnny to stay out of trouble. Well, Johnny says he's a communist and he doesn't believe in property. You can't be angry with Johnny. It's a waste of time.

"Oh you hated Johnny. Was afraid he'd get away. I tried to keep you in good with Johnny. You know Johnny when he gets mad. Just because Johnny warned you not to, you're going down there, aren't you? You remember Johnny? Johnny Boy, your kid brother? This thing of ours? I told Johnny the only reason I was marrying him was because I was tired of waiting for you.

"Really? Then you know Johnny. Why would you say Johnny? You hate Johnny. You've been jumping around Johnny like a trained monkey. You haven't done everything Johnny knows how to do. Johnny doesn't think it would be a tragedy if you lost me.

"Johnny has a job. He couldn't have been at the races. I may have misjudged Johnny. He can be sweet. So protective. Johnny never takes anything seriously, running about the country, getting married here, there, and the other place. Here's my plan. I will get back my empire from Johnny. Someway. Somehow. Johnny has to die, first.

"More money? I never asked Johnny for money. How can I get Johnny to give up gambling? Was Johnny in the car? It was Johnny. You know we can't hide anything from Johnny. Johnny's a nervous wreck anyway. I was talking to Johnny, then fell asleep. I didn't mean to. Johnny was right. We're on the wrong side."

"Look's like Johnny's here. Johnny just hasn't learned, when you're dead lie down. Would you mind? I want to speak to Johnny alone. You heard what Johnny said. No part of the waterfront'll be safe for you now."

2.

"How you feeling, Johnny? Happy birthday, Johnny. Hi, Johnny. Where you been? Johnny, I've been looking for you. Say it! Can't you say something? Please, Johnny. I won't get on your back. What do you want me to do, Johnny?

"Still the hardman, huh, Johnny? Easy as an apple now, Johnny. Watch your smoke, Johnny. Sit down, Johnny. It's nice to be nice, Johnny. Don't worry, Johnny. I'm not here to settle old scores. I hate this, Johnny. I really do. I hate violence. It was rude of you to run away without saying goodbye. It's good to hear your voice, Johnny. It's been a long time. The world has changed, Johnny. You wouldn't believe how much the world has changed.

"What are you doing in this miserable gully, Johnny-my-love? Johnny, it's too dangerous for you to be in public. I want to know how you been, Johnny. It's been a long time since you disappeared, Johnny. You got any friends, Johnny? Which side are you on today, Johnny? Did you ever think of settling down in one place, Johnny?

"Johnny, I want to talk to you a minute. I've given you a couple of chances. I don't know what you're after. Johnny. Why did you leave? Just that one question. Answer me that. Look, I'm sorry, Johnny. You know as well as I do that if I wanted you dead, you'd be dead. Did you ever love a woman, Johnny? I mean, really love her? Have you been bad, Johnny? Have you been bad with other girls?

"Johnny, remember the night? Johnny. It's my fault. There's been a screw-up. Johnny, I knew their secrets. I was just on my way up, Johnny.

"Oh, it's just Johnny, now? We don't get that out here in Newark, Just-Johnny. What's your deal, Just-Johnny? You changed your name and thought you changed everything. Do you know what color my eyes are, Johnny? What're you rebelling against, Johnny? Where in the hell are you from anyway, Johnny? You haven't changed at all, Johnny.

"Johnny, I don't understand. What made you do all this? No, Johnny. I cannot operate without a drink! Johnny, wait a minute. Can't you stop this? Johnny, please! We've been over that! He's sweet, but it was so, innocent! You'd better watch your mouth, Johnny! That's what I love about you, Johnny. You are just as sharp as a razor. Lay off, Johnny. You've enough on your hands for one day. Johnny, why don't you get rid of the grief you got for that blonde, whoever she is.

"Oh, I'm sorry, Johnny. I know that had to hurt. I guess that squares us, Johnny. No, Johnny. Please, don't. Johnny, I'm in a state tonight. I don't know why. I want to be alone. Johnny, where are you going?

"Now look, Johnny. Out there I think you got me wrong. I've got a job to do here, but I'm not hard to get along with. You've been havin' yourself a time, huh, Johnny? Well done, Johnny. Another soul saved from eternal damnation. You really think those people out there care about you? You're just a fad to them, Johnny!

"Johnny, really, you are the limit. How can you be so gay about something you should be ashamed of? Sorry, Johnny. You hear stories.

"Johnny, you finally did something for me. Look, Johnny, don't it look elegant? That's beautiful, Johnny. Do you really mean it, Johnny? Johnny, you're a genius. Johnny, I can't tell you how much that means to me. Johnny, I'm just beginning to understand you. You're a baby. Come on, Johnny, let's go have a beer and I'll beat the living Christmas out of you. Let's go some place. Let's get out of here. Every time you look around, there's cops.

"Johnny. What happened to that cop? Let's go give him a bad time.

"Johnny, you mustn't joke with me. I don't know how to flirt. I know, Johnny. I know you want me so bad it's like acid in your mouth. But not this time. You've got that kamikaze look, Johnny. I've seen it before. Oh I love it when you get angry, Johnny. I really do. You're so bestial.

"Johnny, come here. There's something you need to see. Johnny, please! Let me explain. Johnny! Shut up a minute, Johnny. Listen to me. I should have been a better friend. I shoulda stopped you. I shoulda grabbed you by the neck, I shoulda kicked your teeth in. I'm sorry, Johnny.

"Johnny, I've got something to show you.

"Ninety seconds Johnny. That's all I ask for, just 90 seconds of your life, Johnny, that's it. Johnny, I didn't mean to get in your face. Oh, Johnny, a woman's love is like the morning dew: it's as apt to settle on a horse turd as a rose. I love you, Johnny. I've been looking in every ditch from Fresno to here hoping you was dead. Once I would've crawled at your feet just to be close to you, Johnny. I've looked for you in every man I've met. I have waited for you, Johnny. What took you so long?

"Johnny, it's crazy isn't it? You're afraid of me. Well, your philosophy's slightly cockeyed, Johnny, but I like the way you carry your chin. Save me, Johnny. Talk to me, Johnny. Sing me a song. Buy me a beer. Johnny, don't you remember? The last time we went out scrambling? Johnny, you were going to give me that statue? Will you give it to me now? This is different, Johnny. Really different. You're gonna love it. Come on, Johnny. You can do it. Use your arms. Fly like an eagle. Johnny! You're on fire! Come on, Johnny. I'm singing tonight, Johnny. I'm really singing. I'm on the Christmas tree. That's it, Johnny. Go for it. We are gonna ride this all the way, Johnny. You and me. So let's go. They're listening in America, Johnny. Come on, Johnny. Go. Go. Come on, Johnny. Johnny, you'll have to teach me how. Johnny, I can't do that. I can't do that, Johnny. Johnny, I never let anyone kiss me like this before! Johnny, that isn't even decent. I can't do it, Johnny! I'll look ridiculous! Why, it simply isn't done! I'm shaky. I wish I was going someplace, Johnny. Johnny, I love you. Johnny, do you realize the penalty for impersonating an angel?

"But that's what makes it great, Johnny. We can exist on a different plane. We can make our own rules, Johnny. Why be a servant to the law when you can be its master? To us, Johnny! Look. Look at it, Johnny. It's a once in a lifetime opportunity. Honestly, Johnny, you're only good for two things: making music and making love.

"Leave it alone, Johnny. Johnny. What is it with you? You got that look again. Like you're going to tell me something, then you don't.

"You haven't changed at all, Johnny. We can't double-cross him. He wants to spill the whole setup. Johnny, my chin's hanging out right next to yours. How terrible is wisdom when it brings no profit to the wise, Johnny? Listen to yourself, Johnny. You're talking to a tornado.

"You're cockeyed, Johnny! All cockeyed!

"You know, Johnny, when you play solitaire you can only beat yourself. Johnny, there's going to be no more borrowing. Sorry, Johnny, I don't have a dime. Johnny, I still don't understand. Are you broke? Answer me, Johnny. Do it or you're gonna die, Johnny. Johnny, a man can cheat or man cannot cheat. You can't shut me up, Johnny. Not anymore.

"You just tell me the truth, Johnny. Did your parents die in the car accident?

"I hate you too, Johnny. I hate you so much, I think I'm going to die from it. You do hate me, don't you, Johnny? She was my only friend, Johnny. You ruined everything. Why, Johnny? Why, Johnny? Would it interest you to know how much I hate you, Johnny? You're one dead Johnny. That's what you are.

"Johnny, I swear to God, if you open your mouth about any of this.

"Johnny, don't! That's my entire livelihood. Johnny, hand me that bag of money. It was a mistake to send for you, Johnny. Johnny, we better come up with something real quick. There are all sorts of jobs, Johnny. Like acting. And bringing something to life, it's the same thing. That's why you can't get a job acting, Johnny, because you can't feel anything.

"You're not going to use that gun, Johnny. Do you suppose murderers are happy, Johnny? What good did we do? Nothing! We used to do it real good, Johnny. Killing. The memories. They haunt me, Johnny! I had this dream about the devil. He reserved a whole floor of hell just for me, Johnny. What do you think about that? Hey, Johnny, what did that Mexican mean by a sick horse is going to get us? Some men take to a side of killing, Johnny. Just make sure when the killing time comes you're standing on the right side.

"That's better, Johnny. What do I do now, Johnny? You told me to dry my eyes and blow my nose, in that order. All right, Johnny, but what about my money? Johnny, you owe me. I did time for you.

"You know, Johnny, when I was on the inside I used to defend you. I used to say Johnny's okay, Johnny's good, Johnny's a hero. But I was wrong. Johnny, you don't know what a few months in jail can do to you. You get mean in jail, I don't care, Johnny, I really don't care who gets blown up. I might know a few things, might tell you lies, tantalize you a bit. But I really don't care that much.

"Oh Johnny, Johnny, Johnny. How can you sit there playing that dreamy music with me and this? Don't get happy, Johnny. That's why I'm here, Johnny, to kill myself.

"You'd better go, Johnny. Johnny, you're exactly as big as I let you be, and no bigger, and don't forget it, ever. Johnny, I'll see you in the next life! I'll see you in hell, Johnny. I'm out of here, Johnny. I can't be seen with every Stage Door Johnny. Johnny, write my mother a letter and tell her I'm in the can. Good luck, Johnny. Be brave, huh, Johnny. Sorry, Johnny, but it's only business. Bye bye, Johnny. Goodbye, Johnny. I love you. See you later, Johnny. Goodbye. See you around, Johnny. Any last words, Johnny?

"Johnny, you mean you're going to? Johnny, why were you asking all those questions about the poison? Johnny, you were going to kill yourself! Who do you think's gonna pay for the funeral, Johnny? Don't cry, Johnny. We've all done something, Johnny boy. Johnny, if Heaven exists, what would you like to hear God say when you arrive at the pearly gates? Not all of us are dealing with our demons, Johnny. Some of us are the demons. I'm sorry I got you into this, Johnny. No, don't. I didn't know. Don't, Johnny. We're living, Johnny. We're living. So let's make it count. Oh Johnny, but it'll be different now. We'll make it different. Johnny, let's go back. Let's go home and see it all through together. It will work. I know it will. Johnny, please! Do you love me, Johnny?

"Johnny? Hurry, Johnny. They're coming. Do you understand me? This mission is over! Look at them out there! Look at them! If you won't end this now, they will kill you. Is that what you want? It's over, Johnny. It's over! Hey, Johnny, what's the pitch? We leavin'? You were right, Johnny: you can't win no matter what you do. Johnny, you're about to jump out of a perfectly good airplane. How do you feel about that? Johnny, you haven't told us what it's all about.

"Johnny, I'm scared.

"Sit down, Johnny. We've both done a lot of living. The problem is we have to figure out how to do a little more. No, Johnny, no. It's not our war. Come on, Johnny. Let's run away. Do you know the hotel, Johnny? I'm in no hurry. The Earth and the sun and the sky will still be there when we get there, Johnny. Johnny, where we goin'?

"A hero? Did you hear that, Johnny? We've just been pardoned! They've turned us into heroes, Johnny. You got your hat, your badge, and your boots! You got it all, don't you, Johnny? You got everything! You're happy, aren't you, Johnny? Well, I got just the tune that will fit you! Let's do this, Johnny! Don't be late, Johnny. There's no time, Johnny.

"Well, that's my story, Johnny."

Five Minutes to Sexy Hair

First, know the warning sounds. When sexy hair is *expected* the sirens will emit a rising and falling note. This warning will also be broadcast on the radio:

"Five minutes to sexy hair. I repeat, five minutes to sexy hair."

When sexy hair is *imminent*, the sirens will emit a steady note. Broadcasts will inform you:

"Sexy hair in one minute. I repeat, sexy hair in one minute."

If you are at home, you should send the children as far away from the sexy hair as possible. Turn off the gas and electricity at the mains; turn off all pilot lights. Turn off oil supplies. Close stoves and damp down fires. Shut windows and draw curtains.

If you are in the open and sexy hair is only moments away, go immediately to the nearest building. If there is no building nearby, use any kind of cover, or lie flat and cover the exposed skin of the head and hands.

Light and heat from sexy hair will last for up to 20 seconds, but the sexy hair itself may take up to a minute to reach you.

The dangers from sexy hair will be so intense that you may need to stay inside your refuge for at least 48 hours. If you need to go to the lavatory, or to replenish food or water supplies, do not stay outside your refuge for a second longer than is necessary.

After 48 hours the danger from sexy hair will lessen, but you could still be risking your life through exposure to it.

Visits outside the house should at first be limited to a few minutes for essential duties and should be done by people over 30 where possible. They should avoid bringing sexy hair back into the house, keeping separate shoes or boots for outdoors if they can, and always wiping them.

You may have casualties from the sexy hair, which you will have to care for, perhaps for some days, without medical help. If a death occurs while you are confined, place the body in another room and cover it as securely as possible.

Attach identification.

If no instructions have been given within five days, you should temporarily bury the body as soon as it is safe to go out. Remember to mark the spot.

When you hear "All clear," this means there is no longer an immediate danger from sexy hair and you may resume normal activities.

The Lame Shall Enter at Five Miles Per Hour

1.

"You don't ever want to go to the IHOP on Grand," Len announced with a chop of his hand. "It's a franchise. Those franchise goofs can do whatever they want. No respect for the brand. When I went there I thought it was okay. It's closer to my house. But then I looks at my bill and have to tell the girl, 'I always get the Smokehouse combo. It's $6.40 with my senior's discount, which isn't here.' And you know what she says to me? 'You don't look like a senior.' Me. A 72-year-old man! So she comes back with a form that says the customer requested the senior's discount and would I please sign. I ain't signing that!"

"Don't sign that," I parroted.

"So I leave my $6.40 and never go back."

Len pushed his half-eaten Smokehouse combo away and zipped up his blue track jacket, covering the tufts of white hair escaping his shirt collar. "I like this one," he said tapping the table, "but it's cold in here. They do that in the spring. Too cheap to turn the heat on." He looked back up at me. "What are you, buddy?"

Recently disabled, I thought to myself. I rubbed my leg, tapped my steel knee cap. It was still foreign to me.

But Len clarified his question: "Thirty-nine? Forty?"

"Forty. You're good, Len."

"Best 4-wheel electric scooter dealer in the state."

Len stood up, grasping the banquette and plucking his cane in one unified motion. I took my straight-arm crutches and fell into them like a failed trust exercise. Our waitress ran over and steadied me. "Need some help to the door, hon?" she cooed.

"Thanks, but I'll manage."

As Len and I hobbled and lurched to the door he leaned in, shoulder close. "You idiot. She was rubbing her tsistskehs in your face. A few more feet and you would have got her number." I laughed as Len held the door open for me. "You're laughing because you think it's over. So a car fell on your legs while you were making nine bucks an hour to change oil. Big deal. Those crutches on you are better than a bank full of retirement bonds. Seriously, you get a little more gray I'll introduce you to some guys I know. They only cruise the Alzheimer fun-run circuit for guilt-ridden daughters. So easy."

Outside, we wobbled in front of our rides in silence. Len's was a cherry red Shoprider Sprinter XL4. He obviously junked the original electrical for a Sento 54T engine and a nitrous oxide injection system done up to look like an oxygen tank. Everything was street-illegal save for the wicker basket. Top speed with the nitrous: probably a mean 28 mph.

I sat down on my stock blue Sunrunner 44 and snapped in my crutches. Top speed: 5 mph. Len sat down on the Sprinter, opened the throttle and pushed a hidden kick-starter. His scooter purred. "Life breaks us, buddy, but there's always this." Len ripped the throttle again, sending a rattle through his hollow body and up to his oversized polarized sunglasses. "You know, I've got a thing with some of my preferred clientele. You're a little young but we need more mechanics. You should come by tonight. Estelle's making kugel."

The week before I had purchased the Sunrunner at Len's shop. Every day since, I rode past the IHOP looking for Len, waiting for an in, a wave of familiarity to take me away from daytime TV and dreams of lawsuits I couldn't afford.

2.

"We don't get a lot of crips like you," Len laughed as I struggled out of my scooter. "You'll be our token for the night."

The ride to the empty lot in the city's west end took me two lonely hours and one battery change. A stock scooter was all Medicaid would pay for.

"Give me your hand," he half laughed, reaching out as I finished making my way onto the ground. "Let's walk like a couple of young bucks for a while."

The lot was a fenced-in concrete slab that was at least five acres in length. "Old GM plant," Len told me, "Best run in the city until you hit some I-beams about half way down. We call it MidLife Crisis Point. Of course, nothing like this one track that the Mormons control on the Bonneville flats. Pristine lake bed, but only Mormons allowed. Not even real fucking elders."

Though the races were still an hour away, the scooters began arriving. Machines that blended into the background of any street only a few hours before, draped with plastic bags and novelty flags, now took on the gleam of chariots in the midnight sodium vapor light. Neon detailing was switched on. Headlamps were polished. Pictures of grandchildren were handed around along with bottles of malt liquor. A group of Latino men were testing out hydraulics that bounced their scooters up and down. One was cut so low its frame showered sparks as a driver fishtailed it. "I'll take some heat for having you around," Len warned as we walked the pits and old clouded eyes stared me down. "We're mostly hip cases here. Some diabetes and gout. The problem is, when you're as young as you are, old timers just think you're a druggie. Incidentally, I can score some morphine off a friend of mine with bowel—"

"It's all right. But I'm going to sit down for the concert," I said as I fell back into my scooter. "Sure are some nasty machines here, Lenny."

"Should be. They're all mine. Look." Len cocked his head towards the gates, "Competition is here." Driving in a diamond formation was a group of Chinese senior citizens. They all wheezed down to breaking, save the scooter in the front, which continued on towards us. The driver—in golf coat, baseball cap, and lap blanket—hit the brakes only an inch in front of Len, who put his arms on the handlebars and pushed feebly. "Ready to get your ass smeared on the track, Chen Chi Li? Just like I did to you in St. Petersburg."

"Len," Chen Chi Li drawled out. "Stick to the mahjong. Like the other old ladies."

Len struck his cane against Chen Chi Li's front bumper. "All right. Either we race now or you turn your Golden Tech around, and go back to Casino Rama, where your son thinks you are."

Chen Chi Li stared at Len, let out a low chortle, and backed his scooter away.

3.

I lined up on along the racetrack, a big gap between myself and the pit crews. At the starting line, Len, Chen Chi Li, and a second stringer named Barry primped and adjusted their scooters. A man as old as a twisted branch and in a pale blue cardigan shuffled on a walker out in front of the racers. He held a white hanky in his hand, ready to start the race.

"Does your mother know you're out this late?" came a woman's voice behind my ear.

I turned around, almost speechless in front of a shock of silver white hair, pale skin, and wide, sly lips. "Does Lauren Bacall know you're going to put her out of business?" I replied. The flirt startled her and she backed her scooter away with a short zoom sound. She brushed her hair and I saw a diamond earring that matched the necklace that ran across her black blouse.

"You're a little young to be running with this crowd, aren't you?" she said, composing herself.

"You're a little too showroom to be running with this crowd, aren't you?"

"I believe the boys are starting to play," she said, pointing to the racetrack.

At the starting line, the scooters revved. The starter took his hanky, blew his nose in it. He looked at what came out before remembering his job, saying, "Oh, okay." The starter held the hanky aloft again.

"I didn't even hear your scooter come up behind me," I said to her.

"Well, my husband—*Leonard*—maintains a machine very well. My name's Estelle and you are the new mechanic, I assume." We shook hands. "Pretty skin for a mechanic. Sure you're not a Harvard boy?"

The hanky dropped and the electric scooters tore out, first at five, then 10, and then 15 miles per hour, flickering under the lamps like a yellowed filmstrip. Estelle could feign boredom with the races but she couldn't hide her smile as Len, his white hair and polar fleece jacket blowing in the air, shot out almost to the lead, just behind Barry. Yet as Len was reaching for his nitrous release, Barry let go of his handlebars, clutched his chest and threw his head back. His scooter weaved. Chen Chi Li went off to the side, driving safely into the spin. Len sideswiped Barry's motorized cadaver at 15 miles per hour. It was almost dangerous. Estelle grabbed my leg. She gasped. I winced and I liked it. That was outright dangerous.

Everyone on the sidelines wheeled out. Chen Chi Li was searching for his hat. Len got out of his scooter and looked down at Barry. "Heart disease is the number one killer in America and the moron misses his meds again," he lamented as Estelle minced out of her scooter and grabbed him.

"You stupid man," she said, nuzzling her face into his neck.

I zoomed over to Len's scooter. Front right tire flat. Axle maybe cracked. I ran my hand over the front—definite filler and paint job needed.

Len shouted, "Guess my new mechanic is going to come by tomorrow and show his stuff? Do me a favor, kid. Hitch that wreck to the back of Estelle's scooter for me. My arms are killing me."

"What about Barry?"

"What about him? He was 76 years old. Died like a damn Apache out there." Len rubbed his wrinkled face. "You ever see the inside of a rest home?" Estelle turned Len away while he was still talking. "Some of the boys'll drop Barry off at a bus stop. Don't worry—worst that'll happen is an op-ed about seniors and public transit."

4.

My Sunrunner pushed through the morning rain as I drove over to Len's house while rivulets of water dripped down my poncho. Len's house was a ranch style at the end of a suburban cul-de-sac. As I whizzed up to the covered front porch I saw Estelle draped against the door in a robe, hair pulled back, holding a glass of prune juice—a ghost fox.

"You missed him. I finally got him to go to the doctor's about his arm. The old fool." I stood in the rain with all my weight on the crutches. She beckoned with her hand. "It's okay. You can hang out with the boss's wife."

Inside I sat down on the plastic-covered couch, my soaked body sliding around. "Now I know why Len did that to our furniture," she quipped before floating into another room. She came back with a towel. I grabbed the towel but she wouldn't let go. We tugged and giggled. We dropped it on the orange shag carpet. The house was museum quality 1970s.

"I'm 25 years older than you. Old enough to be—"

"Old enough to have been my young, irresponsible mother," I finished. "Times change, Estelle, women's expectations of themselves are different. You can't use the mother argument unless you're 30 to 40 years older these days."

"You seem well practiced at flattering older ladies."

"I'm just a fast learner," I replied before my knee spasmed with pain and I flew back on the couch with a crinkling plastic sound.

Estelle turned around towards the bathroom, "I'll get you some naproxen."

She came back with two pills and water. She sat down next to me and took my leg carefully across her lap. "You move pretty good for someone who drives a scooter," I said.

"My mornings are better. But I was lucky. My doctors only re-finished my hip socket—not a total replacement. But Len," she said with a sigh. "Len is more like one of his machines now, the way they work on him."

"What about that guy Barry? A man dies and you two treat it like your Azeala just didn't make it."

Estelle rubbed my leg. "At this age, it is about the same. Do you know what his last name was? It was White."

"Funny."

"And he was checking the mail 50 times a day by last week. Sometimes in the middle of the night."

I felt the medication working and the tension around my knee go down. I sat up and the couched plastic screamed. "You're a little too smart for us gear heads."

"I was a dancer. Modern, actually. I opened The Kitchen in New York in '71. My performance was about the table of the elements. Iron was represented by a forward digging motion." Estelle glared straight ahead and moved her hands like she was clawing air dirt and we both laughed. "Everything else, I forget. Helium might have been a slow rise with shaking hands—anyway, darling, a dancer's joints are dead by 40. I moved out here with my sister and taught at the college. After the surgery, I started saving my pills up, waiting for the night when I just couldn't take it anymore, but then I met Len." Len, owner of Electricscooterland. *All health insurance plans honored.* "He promised me mobility and freedom." Her finger traced my leg and she repeated in a whisper, "And freedom."

I put my hand up to her face, brushed it with my knuckles and moved it around her neck. I brought Estelle towards me. I kissed her mouth and the thin skin of her face. I pulled open her sash and slid my hands under her robe. Her body was like paper on top of me. She pulled back and took down my pants. I winced. "Take this leg," I wheezed, pointing to my scarred left knee, "and move it straight out."

Estelle did, and smiled. "I have to be on top of you." She pointed a finger to a faded scar on her left hip, "and this leg has to stay straight." She straddled me and together we were a perfect match of broken pieces of flesh and cobalt. We moved in waves of couch plastic crinkling and clicking.

5.

Len came back into the house and found me drinking coffee in his Barcalounger, my leg floating at full extension. At the same moment Estelle walked into the living room with Windex and paper towel in hand to wipe away my ass- and thigh-shaped condensation off the plastic. We all stood there, knowing, before Len said, "I'm going out to the garage before humidity hits 100. Coming, Buddy?" Out in Len's garage the last of the rain ran down the open door. After we finished putting the new front axle on, Len pushed a button, his hand trembling with a slight palsy, and the hydraulic lift let his scooter down. I wobbled over to the tub of Fast Orange, brought the plunger down, and whipped the grease and grit into a citrus froth.

Len looked adoringly at his scooter, "I'll have to bring it into the paint shop next week but let's test her."

"Around the block?" I asked.

"You kids waste every day, don't you? Might as well make an IHOP run. You can take Estelle's ride." Len paused, swallowed and clenched his jaw. "If you think you can handle it. It's got a Kaishon 500 W. Not as much torque as mine but it'll let you keep up, if I play nice."

In the driveway I sat down on Estelle's scooter and caught her scent—rose, cough drops, and expensive leather. I brushed the steering column lightly with my knuckles. Len revved his engine and circled around me. "Come on," he winked. "Let's do street."

Len tore out and I followed close behind, his glass pack muffler shredding my ears. We left the cul-de-sac, Len taking sharp weaves like a child with a new bike, speeding up anytime I would get close. We turned down Grand and past the franchise IHOP run by goofs, Len surging his scooter and cutting off a car exiting the parking lot. I spun around the car close enough I could've slapped the hood.

Len let loose on an open stretch of the road, making it up to 30 miles per hour. I pushed Estelle's scooter as fast as it could go. Len was still ahead. The good IHOP was off the next left but Len veered up an expressway offramp. I stopped and watched, my eyes following in shock as Len and his scooter drove, between lanes, against the cars honking and pulling over to the side of an overpass.

Len raised one arm up into the air, fist clenched, and threw his head back. Cars continued to pull over for him in an impromptu game of chicken.

I watched until his heat-blurred Shoprider disappeared into a vanishing point of freedom and mobility.

Untitled Senator Joseph Lieberman
Vanity Film Project

FROM THE DESK OF SENATOR JOSEPH LIEBERMAN

The movie takes place in two parts, modeled on the Old and New Testaments. The first half opens with Joseph Lieberman—dressed in black leather—and his naked son riding a horse across a desert. During their journey, they find a blood-drenched adobe village with all the inhabitants dead and mutilated. Joseph Lieberman avenges the townsfolk by hunting down and killing the outlaws who butchered them. Joseph Lieberman discovers that the outlaws are under the command of a colonel who has taken another village hostage. Joseph Lieberman rescues the town from the colonel, only to abandon his son with local monks in order to ride off with a woman the colonel held captive. Joseph Lieberman names her Mara after the bitter water they later drink from a pond. Mara then convinces Joseph Lieberman to defeat the four gun masters of the desert in order to become the greatest gunman ever.

The first duel is with a blind man dressed in only a thong and guarded by a man with no legs riding a man with no arms. After that battle an unnamed woman with a male voice finds Joseph Lieberman and Mara and offers to lead them to the next master. The second master is accompanied by his mother and a lion while the third is found at a rabbit farm. After battling and traveling through the desert, Joseph Lieberman comes to the final gun master. Joseph Lieberman wishes to duel but the man says he has no pistol, having traded it away years ago for a butterfly net. The two start a fistfight where Joseph Lieberman is unable to connect a single blow. Frustrated, Joseph Lieberman attempts to shoot the man, who catches the bullets in his butterfly net and throws them back at the bipartisan politician. Realizing that he is finally beaten, Joseph Lieberman submits to death but the master asks if his life is really worth taking. The master then takes the pistol away from Joseph Lieberman and kills himself in a demonstration of the unimportance of life.

Filled with madness and guilt, Joseph Lieberman destroys his own gun. The unnamed woman then confronts Joseph Lieberman and shoots him multiple times, inflicting Christ-like wounds on his hands and feet. The women ride off together, leaving Joseph Lieberman to die in the desert. The first half ends with Joseph Lieberman being taken away by a band of deformed beggars.

The second half of the movie takes place years later. The outcasts have secreted the senator to their city inside a mountain where, comatose, he's tended to by a female dwarf. When Joseph Lieberman awakes, he shaves off his pubic hair and dons the simple clothing of an ascetic. He pledges to help lead the crippled outcasts out of their mountain refuge, and, together with the dwarf, goes to a nearby town to raise money to buy dynamite and tools.

Once they arrive, they find that the citizens of the town are corrupt capitalists who hold blood sports, trade in slaves, and indulge in odd sexual pleasures. A mysterious monk also arrives in town to lead the failing local Christian church.

While earning money doing odd jobs around the town, Joseph Lieberman and the dwarf are forced at gunpoint to have sex in front of a crowd of drunken, hooting capitalists. While making love, the dwarf reveals that she is in love with Joseph Lieberman but she is ashamed of her body. Joseph Lieberman convinces her that she is beautiful and asks for her hand in marriage. At the church the new priest reveals that he is indeed Joseph Lieberman's abandoned son and then threatens to shoot Joseph Lieberman but is stopped by the dwarf because she needs Joseph Lieberman to save her people.

The son of Joseph Lieberman, now dressed in the black leather of his father's past, decides to spare Joseph Lieberman's life until he finishes digging the exit for the crippled people of the mountain. The trio work together to build a tunnel and in the process become a family.

The opening is completed and the people hobble out of the mountain while Joseph Lieberman cries after them, "They are not ready for you!" The people arrive at the town, but the capitalists are waiting with guns. Joseph Lieberman witnesses his adopted community cut down by bullets and, in trying to save them, is himself shot several times. In a fit of rage, Joseph Lieberman takes a shotgun and kills every capitalist in town: men and women, old and young. In the midst of this the dwarf gives birth. Joseph Lieberman then douses his wounded body in oil, assumes a lotus position, and sets himself alight.

Joseph Lieberman's adult son, the dwarf, and the infant all survive the battle and ride off on a horse in the same fashion as at the beginning of the film.

Voice Over

1.

A story of two people. Two lovers you'll never forget, two amazing secret agents. Two worlds, one love, two brothers, one gangster, and the most heinous of crimes. One diabolical madman, five suspects, two lovers. One killer, two women, one man, one man's dream, one woman's obsession. A lady of the night. A man of the cloth. It took them 17 years to learn the rules, and one week to break them all. One man's dilemma in a small town desperate for hope. One family, one murder, too many lies. One cop is too hot, one cop is too cool; one fights for justice, the other for power. Only one can survive one night of ecstasy and a lifetime of sorrow. One good cop. One bad cop. One very dangerous woman. A one-armed man. Two sisters. Two lives. One loves. One hunts. One doesn't count, the other can't. One seduces. One kills. One wants to love. Two men enter. One man leaves.

Two identical strangers. Two different worlds. One perfect match. A socialite. A runaway. A fatal meeting. Two people, one mystery, one thing in common—two heads grafted to the body of a giant. One's a dreamer, one's a schemer, and together they're on the run and layin' low. 100 Assassins. 1,000 Weapons. 10,000,000 Dollars. Two apartments. Two women. One shocking mystery. A thousand hours of hell for one moment of love. Five taxis. Five cities. One night. One con out to save his million-dollar scam, one priest out to save his only brother, two women, and one tropical island. One's hot. One's cool. They're both boiling mad. One broke his silence. The other broke the system. No one would take on his case until one man was willing to take on the system. Five terrorists. One kid. Two different worlds. One true love. Two tiny mice, one big adventure. Four perfect killers. One perfect crime. Two different worlds. Only one is real.

The story of one outrageous woman caught between two men. One's a warrior. One's a wiseass. One girl. Two guys. Three possibilities. They're two L.A. cops going after a gang of drug lords. Two young heroes. One small town. Five strangers. Four secrets. Three schemes. Two best friends. Two captains. One destiny. Six hundred lives, one directive. One man's vision of utopia, one man's search for peace, and one woman's search for her lost son. Two friends. One past. No future. Both of them certain of one thing—a story of two people.

2.

She's 10 miles of bad road for every hood in town. They say she kissed 2,000 men. She's a one-mama massacre squad. She'll put you in traction. She forced an entire lifetime of passion into one lust-filled summer. Tonight she will love again and kill again. Her beauty is a dangerous weapon of war. Her passion for art changed the face of history. She's brown sugar and spice but if you don't treat her nice she'll put you on ice. Mistress of the waterfront, she was too much for one town, and no town would have her. No man could tame her. She's a love-starved moon maiden, on the prowl blasting Nazis on a bold commando raid and finding love in precious, stolen moments. As a lawyer, all she wanted was the truth. As a daughter, all she wanted was his innocence. She's 15. The only adult she admires is Johnny Rotten. She lives. Don't move. Don't breathe. She will find you. Could she kill and kiss and not remember?

On the naked stage she has no secrets. When she shimmied, the whole world shook. When she sang, the whole world thrilled. She steals his car and his furniture. But can she steal his heart? She scorched her soul to save an American cavalry officer. Here she is, that eye-filling, gasp-provoking blonde bombshell. The man-by-man story of a lost soul. Every time she says, "I love you," she breaks the law.

Just when she met the man of her dreams, along came her husband to ruin everything. She was at the head of the line, in a place she didn't belong, in a fight no one thought she could win. They gave her a bad name and she lived up to it. Every man who sees her digs her, but she digs kicks of a very special kind. He was 15. She was 40. The only thing she couldn't remember was how to forget. Feared by every man, desired by every woman, she's so hot, you'll need to call 911. In a world of power and privilege, one woman dared to obey her heart.

She's so romantic she drives four men frantic. She went for anything in pants. She was born outside the laws of god and man. She called it an accident, the headlines shrieked "Murder!" She heard herself convicted by the man she loved.

What strange power made her half woman and half snake? She was a starlet out to make the big time—the men, the passions, the lonely nights—until she found fulfillment in a sunlit paradise. She's given up on love but love hasn't given up on her, because wanting a man dead can be reason enough to live. She gave them what they wanted and they took everything she had. She's 200 pounds of maniacal fury. Too young to know, too wild to care, too eager to say, "Yes." She lived and loved like the violent jungle around her.

She'd wink till hearts went on the blink and staid professors couldn't think. And everywhere they'd stop to stare. Fame. Be careful. It's out there for a girl whose life is not what she believes it to be. No force could sway her. No fear could stop her. She brought a small town to its feet and a huge corporation to its knees. They gave her looks, brains, nuclear capabilities—everything but an "off switch." Its creator made it in her own image. The military made it deadly. Now only one man can stop her. Once you cross this special agent, you've crossed the line and discovered the stark naked truth of a woman's desire for love. Daring. Revealing. Shocking. Goddess of love in a city of sin. She ain't mama's little girl no more—a wrong girl from the right side of the tracks, made of fire and ice, and everything dangerous. "Sure, I accept favors from men," she said.

She's not a pickup or a pushover—she's more dangerous than either. Something happens when she hears the music. It's her freedom. It's her fire. It's her life. Between the terror outside her door and the horror inside her mind, you have to get out of her life if you want to stay alive. Motorcycle mama on a highway to hell. Leather on the outside. All woman on the inside. What must a good girl say to "belong?"

She was all he had left between San Quentin and death row. She learned about men from him. She played the age-old game of love like there'd be no tomorrow.

She was born to be bad, to be kissed, to make trouble. The only thing she wanted to take on her honeymoon was her boyfriend. She made good—with a plunging neckline and the morale of a tigress. She knows all about love potions, and lovely motions. The American girl, victim of Berlin's political intrigue—she dared—the only thing hotter than her dreams is reality. She's an undercover cop, seduced by a fantasy, trapped in a mystery, led by a dangerous impulse. She came to the edge of the world to find something more, but through one indiscretion, a woman with a future became a woman with a past. Her lovers went from bed, to dead. Renegade woman—tough as they come. The adventure, the ecstasy, the supreme suspense of a woman wronged beyond words, almost beyond revenge. Mistress of an empire of savages and beasts; intelligence was her crime, intolerance her enemy. Bad men gave her a name that the Panhandle spoke only through gunsmoke.

She broke the rules, and changed their lives. A cheat at heart, from her painted toes to her plunging neckline, a good girl until she lights a "reefer." Perfect girl. Car crazy. Speed crazy. Boy crazy. Her soft mouth was the road to sin-smeared violence. Loving him was easy. Trusting him was deadly. She made a career out of love. She made the frozen north red hot. She blew the lid off the wild west. Her treachery stained every stone of the pyramid. Look if you like, but look out. She's man bait, and in the heart of this young woman lies a secret that divides a nation. Hers was the deadliest of the seven sins. What she needs, money can't buy. She's spying on two strangers. She's about to murder her best friend and she's only 16 years old. She led three strange lives. Which was her real self?

Eight years ago she lost her memory, now a detective must help her remember the past before it buries them both. She'll coax the blues right out of your heart. Let her show you the heat of desire, the face of sin. Her dreams inspired hope. Her words inspired passion. Her courage forged a nation's destiny. Torn from her arms, a child of love a woman can give but once. She rules a palace of pleasure . . . for women. Where men are used in a diabolical plot to destroy civilization. The slick chicks who fire up the big wheels. The gayest girlie spree of all time. Untamed girls of the pack-gang. Girls from the "right" kind of home stumbling into the "wrong" kind of love. Bored, thrill-hungry, they shop for sin. Super sisters on cycles, these women carry guns. They dare to do what other women only dream about.

Their law is the whip. Their trademark the branding iron. Better move your butt when these ladies strut. They play around with murder like they play around with men. Meet those not-so-sainted sisters. See women who use the love machine to allay the male shortage. Three foxy mamas turned loose, they can lick any man ever made. Guts as hard as the steel of their hogs, riding their men as viciously as they ride their motorcycles. Scarlet women out to get every thrill they could steal. The wildest girl gang that ever blasted the streets, joined together, how can they make love to separate husbands?

She didn't take orders. She took over. She's not just getting married, she's getting even. She was everything the west was— young, fiery, exciting. She went to sleep as a secretary and woke up a madman's "bride." She's about to bare her soul and all that goes with it. They shattered her world. Now she's out for justice. And vengeance. Only a nervy girl succeeds in a game of death where men fail. She was sent back in time to ensure the future of mankind. She's never been hip. Never been cool. Never been in. Until now. Model, pop star, goddess, junkie, icon—heaven was in her eyes and her lips were paradise. Queen of the outlaws, queen of sin. A date. A drink. A car. A kiss. Now she's known as "that girl."

Schoolgirl by day. Hollywood hooker by night. Her only chance for the future is to embrace the power of her past. Into the land of the lawless rode a blonde wildcat. The gal who invented love. Gungirl. Untamed. Unashamed. She brought danger, death, and desire to the west. A six-gun siren who shoots to thrill, with tricky eyes, dangerous smile, and exquisite gowns. Nimble fingers. He strayed and he paid—she saw to that. She was prepared for anything, until love stormed in. Her name is about all you can handle. You call her a "playgirl" but this girl plays for keeps. She created a monster as her secret lover. She was everything they dreamed of and nothing they expected.

The strange love life of a wrestling gal. Charlie, Sidney, Roger. The names and places didn't matter—only *when*. Dance she did, and dance she must—between her two loves. Caged boy-hungry wildcat gone mad. A white-hot story of a good girl in a bad world. A vision of beauty born in hell, she gave and gave, until she had nothing left to give. The low-down story of a high-class gal who became a national pastime. The chauffeur's daughter who learned her stuff in Paris. She challenged the desert, its men, their passions, and ignited a bold adventure. Born to shop, she learned to kill. The seals have been broken. The prophecies have begun. Now only one woman can halt the end of our world.

It's a crime what prison can do to a girl. Every mom wants to be wanted, but not for murder one. Love's a dangerous game, where a woman's beauty is the pawn of sinister, clutching hands. She wrote the book on love. She will never be free, until she unlocks her past. She who must be obeyed. She who must be loved. She who must be possessed. The weird, wondrous story of the beautiful woman who bathed in flame and lived 500 years, at last to find her first love at this very hour. The story of a woman who raised havoc with a dozen lovers. She wrote the year's blushing best-seller, then had to live it, page by burning page. No one thought she had the courage, the nerve, or the lingerie. Gorgeous gal who set the Ozarks on fire.

Smart about everything, except men. Love wrecked, the flower of southern chivalry dewed with the shining glory of a woman's tears. A top cop torn between her heart and her badge. Meet that guild gal, she gives as good as she gets. The shock-by-shock confessions of a sorority girl—smart, pretty, and all bad.

Meet the gayest lady who ever went to town. She made plowboys into playboys. Her machete isn't her only weapon. Hungry female: a man never tasted that good. She'll make you join the sexual liberation army. She corrupted the youthful morality of an entire school. Her best lessons were taught after class. The men in her life sometimes lived to regret it. While some women are waiting to exhale, this one is ready to get even. Her mission—seduce and destroy. Her deadliest weapon—her body. Lips that kissed more men than she could remember also crooned lullabies no one could forget. She had other weapons besides guns and used them. Every man was her target. She's the girl with the power to turn you on and to turn you off.

3.

His story is written in bullets, blood, and blondes. He keeps human life in test tubes, and prowls at night in the skin of an ape. He was a two-fisted, singing sea ranger. His body is an empty shell that hides a lustful fiend. He played the game of love like it was Russian roulette. For the girl of his dreams, he'd make a deal with the devil. They stole his mind, now he wants it back. Half-man, half-demon, half-insect, half-crazed, half-corpse, half-beast. He is afraid. He is alone. He is three million light years from home. In order to catch him, he must become him.

He was born to rule a world of ancient tradition. Nothing prepared him for our world of change. He left behind everything he knew for the only thing he ever wanted. He's a big-city kid in a small town. He thought there was nothing more seductive than money. The way he practices law should be a crime. He sees their faces. He feels their pain. He touches their lives. They'd never forget the day he drifted into town. He's so far undercover he may never get back. Through miles of raging ocean he defined man's law. Falsely accused. Wrongly imprisoned. He fought for justice to clear his father's name. He knew the risks. He's here and he wants to clean up the town. Searching for glory, he found hell. Born to poverty. Destined for stardom. God made him simple. Science made him a god. Now, he wants revenge.

The touching story of a boy and his right hand. Deadliest hands of kung fu, longest arm of the law. Tortured by desires his vows forbid, master of a house of mortal sin. To thwart a king's passion, he gambled the fate of a nation. They sabotaged his nuclear lab. They took his wife. They tried to kill him. Then they cloned him. He was a man who couldn't care less, until he met a man who couldn't care more.

He hit "the Man" for $3 million. Right where it hurts. In the diamonds. And baby, that's cold. Save your lipstick, girls, he plays for keeps. Dealer. Snitch. Junkie. Hustler. Suddenly, life was more than French fries, gravy, and girls. He's a big city plastic surgeon in a small town that doesn't take plastic. The black cat from Watts. The kung fu cat from Hong Kong. Delightfully devilish, definitely deadly. Every kiss carved his name on another bullet. It took him 20 years to find out who he was and two laps to let the world know. He was the lord of 10,000 years, the absolute monarch of China. He's on the right side of justice, but the wrong side of the law. Indecent. Immoral. Irresistible. It's the role he was born to play. Singing six-guns that sang a song of death for the gang that was out to frame him. He's lost his car. He's lost his money. He's lost his girlfriend. Now he's losing his mind. Boy, oh boy. What you can see thru his X-ray specs?

Lord high minister of everything sinister. He's on a mission so secret, even *he* doesn't know about it. He was an innocent from a small village, soon to be trapped in the erotic underworld of Prague. Women want him for his wit. The CIA wants him for his body. Real badge. Real gun. Fake cop. When he's around, nothing adds up. He planned a paradise. He created a hell. The truth is more shocking than the uniform he wears. Everything that makes him dangerous makes her love him more. A man of evil with a face that could stop a heart and eyes that crawl with madness and hands that creep like cobras. He frees hostages for a living. Now he's taking hostages to survive. Trying to kill him was their first mistake. Letting him live was their last. Tonight, he either fights for his life or he'll be running for the rest of it.

He knew where $50,000 lay begging to be stolen. He took them all on. On their terms. On their turf. Your singin', fist-swingin', cowboy favorite. You may not like what he does, but are you prepared to give up his right to do it? His secret power menaced the world. The ghost who walks. The man who cannot die. He sold his soul for rock and roll. The crowd worshipped him, one woman understood him. Country's biggest star. He'd trade it all to find the kind of love he'd only sung about. No man, no law, no war can stop him. For years the government paid him to kill. Now he is self-employed. He can turn the simple into the simply amazing, and now he turns revenge into high comedy. They said there wasn't a man in the world who could pull off this job, they were right. He's an astro-not turned astronaut in the maddest mix-up in space history. He lives to kill and kills to live. He's back in the most human heart-warming picture in years. The funny man is here with rhythm, comedy, and music. He's a vampire who hasn't scored in 400 years. The miracle kid with the super zoom ball. He's at it again. Chasing down the most dramatic crime in London legend. Shock-charged drama, with a peppery bit of love on the side. A man without a name can never be identified. A man who doesn't exist can never be caught. A man who doesn't love can never truly be alive. Men call him savage, women call him all the time.

He's fighting a war he doesn't believe in, hoping to find something he does. He loved the American dream. With a vengeance. A secret experiment gave him super senses. Then came the side effects. Some say he's nuts. Some say he's bolts. Sensual. Controversial. Available. Follow his secret from bedroom to bedlam, with guns, girls, and dynamite. A symphony of the range, played with instruments of death. He's on the loose again, and this time he's got his soul brothers with him. Fighting for love and life. Born in darkness. Sworn to justice. Now he's using his skills to help a woman seek revenge against the Miami underworld, with his foot on the gas and no brakes on the fun. In his eyes, the threat of terror. In his hands, the power to destroy. The regeneration of a square-jawed westerner who staked his all on the love of a girl, and won.

The cop who won't stop is back. But this time he's chasing down a lot more than a fugitive. Created of science. Void of soul. Almost human. Almost perfect. Almost under control. He turned the lights off, and the city on. Invincible. Unstoppable. Indestructible. He's out on the street and out of control. He went west into the arms of two women. What is a vow to man or God when two sway in the desert's spell—where none know, none hear, where no prying eyes may see? Suddenly he could see through clothes, flesh, and walls. The world's most private detective.

He lived and died a hundred times, now he has 24 hours to unravel 2,000 years of mystery, dead end jobs, a drunk ex-girlfriend, and psychotic vampires. This tall Texan rides a tank and wears lip gloss. The highest flyin', slickest, meanest dude you'll ever face is on the case. Hunted by 1,000 men, haunted by a lovely girl. They drew first blood, but he's gonna fight back like Billy Jack. Years ago he shattered his life. Now he's back to pick up the pieces. He loses his banana and finds nirvana. Golf pro. Love amateur. His world was silent, his love was computers. His rage was the illness of the times.

He has traveled from a galaxy far beyond our own. He is 100,000 years ahead of us. He has powers we cannot comprehend. And he is about to face the one force in the universe he has yet to conquer. Love.

4.

These two should never have fallen in love. They were hired killers going up against the deadliest force of all—each other. Woman's love, man's hate, blazing romance in a city aflame with carnival pleasures. Here on this nameless island they were *male* and *female*. Nothing else, until the raw wind of jealousy stripped their passions bare. Outnumbered, unarmed, unprepared, the mission was a sham. The murders were real and too thrilling for words, so they set it to music. They were Siamese twins, playthings of desire. Hate was the chain that linked them together. God help the one who broke it. First their love was forbidden by law. Then it was torn apart by war. They hurled back their answer in flesh and flame. A thriller-diller of laffs, lust-mad men, and lawless women in a vicious and sensuous orgy of slaughter and stupendous dance spectacles with hundreds of glorified beauties, staged under water. The civil war made them outlaws. The people made them heroes. The violent frontier's strangest triangle.

Their only crime was curiosity. They wrote the sex manifesto of the free love generation. A gambler who trusted no one. A woman who risked everything for a passion that brought them together in the most dangerous city in the world. He's a cop on the edge. She's a woman with a dangerous secret. And now they're both full of melody, full of young love. Enemies because they were taught to be. Allies because they had to be. They were fighting over a woman when the plane went down. Now, their only chance for survival is each other. It's Yankee ingenuity vs. ruthless red-agent cunning, as the pursuer becomes the pursued in a border-to-Baltic flight for life. Sex-*sationally* different. So frank, so outspoken, so true, we don't dare tell you how daring it is. The wildest, wittiest whirlwind of a love battle. Outrageously racy, gay as champagne. The tops in topsy-turvy romance. What strange law brought this beautiful woman into his cell? The crazed love of a ravishing teenage girl for a prehistoric giant. So daring, so tender, so human. Parents may be shocked, but youth will understand.

5.

The action is go. These are the young and the wanton, the beat, and the bad. Drugs, thugs, and freaked-out starlets, pent up punks on a penthouse binge, daring to live, daring to love, flirting with death. Playing with danger, laughing at life. Before your eyes, flaming youth in a thrill-a-second sensation. So young, so innocent, so deadly. They came to conquer the world in a war of survival against the biker freaks and the dune buggy straights. Slowly and with horror the parents realized their children were the slaves of the things from outer space—the drifters, the hipsters, the hot sisters. Today's big jolt about the beatnik jungle. Here is the truth about today's flappers and lounge lizards. When the ski nicks meet the ski chicks it's called snow-a-go-go.

The free-living world of the over-teens, torn from today's headlines. Throbbing tale of shackled youth. Hot steel between their legs. The kids who live today, as if there's no tomorrow. They had to eat three times their body weight each day, or starve. They live from spinout to crack up, and they love as fast as they can get it. They'll take a curve, any curve. They drive faster, love harder, and swing more than anyone else on earth. Hot rod hotshots and their tailgate babes. The story of today's "get lost" generation, the "sex conscious" generation, the "now" generation. Teenage gangs rip highways and skies with thrills and terror. It's the action you expect from today's "shook-up" kids shaking loose. They jet you where the fun and action are, every time they grab a wheel, or a girl. The no-punches-pulled story of a generation that has torn the word "morals" out of the dictionary. Taste a moment of madness; listen to the sound of purple. Every summer they emerge for a ritual of sex and death. Their guns are hot and their bodies are hard. Proud young rebels, teenage terrorists, tearing up the streets.

Call them punks, call them animals, but you better get out of their way. The story of angry youths who terrorize young innocents. Motorcycle maniacs on wheels, breezy riders roaring to hell. Let the fuzz take you alive, these angels aren't that particular.

Behind these "nice" school walls, a teacher's nightmare, a teenage jungle. A shocking glimpse into the warped morals of the mod world. Sometimes "teenager" is spelled TNT. Youth struts its stuff in gorgeous revue. Sex, drugs, and study hall. A dramatic thunderbolt of modern youth. A caress, an embrace, then defilement and death. Tarnished, tempted, violently thrown aside. Too young to be careful. Too tough to care. Now it's too late to say "no." They all talk, fight, and love just one way: dirty. Their god is speed and they came from beyond the stars to spawn in the sea. Under-aged, over-sexed, kick-happy, thrill-hungry, always reckless and willing. Shock suspense sensation—the truth about revved-up youth on a thrill rampage. See them burst out of their clothes and bust up a town. Thrill-crazed space kids blasting the flesh off humans. Groovy gravy, this trip is out of sight.

6.

The war was over and the world was falling in love again. A thousand voices. A single dream. A raging torrent of emotion that even nature can't control. Far up. Far out. Far more. He kissed her all over the map on another fellow's honeymoon. He was her only weakness, she was his greatest strength. When a handsome devil meets a living angel, it's one hell of a good time. Thrilling as love born amid a thousand fabulous adventures. Romance as glorious as the towering Andes. Each day a rendezvous with peril, each night a meeting in astravision, sexicolor, sensurround-flaming hillbilly color. When the pajama tops meet the pajama bottoms, someone's gonna have a fit. An orgy of looting and lust. Primed to explode . . . on contact. A man, a girl, captives in their own worlds, finding escape in each other. It's a whirlwind of laughter, pathos, and illusion.

7

Hate crawling back from the grave. They rob from the rich and just keep it. Their love was a flame that destroyed. If there was an 11th commandment, they would have broken that, too. They needed help. What they got was a miracle. The jive charmers who turn out the dive-bombers. Meet the boy and girl who are sending for Uncle Sam. He's bad. She's worse. Nothing can tame them and scandal can't shame them. Their enemy gave them no choice: love in despair, die without honor. They are evil. They are dead. They are ravenous, they don't take prisoners. They take lives. Killer to the left, killer to the right, stand up, sit down, fright, fright, fright. So provocative the censors banned it, so powerful it came true. All the more blatant in color.

A man, a girl, and a thousand bolo knives. Always outnumbered. Never outfought. Calm under pressure, cool under fire. A lonely man, a lovely girl, struggling against the secret shadow of a remembered woman who came between their lips, but these two had the courage to hope, and to live their love. Now all they have to fear is each other. Getting steamed up over blondes got them into hot water. Romance on the beam. Rhythm in the groove. Laughs on the loose. All new thrills in a sumptuous portrayal of sensuous society in the perfumed fragrance of Park Avenue and Paris boudoirs. Blazing guns and plunging horses on the canyon trail with gold bullion and a glorious girl as the stakes in a game of courage. It had to be told sooner or later—we're telling it now. A heart-load of maddening beauties in gasping gowns. A fortune in furs. A ransom in jewels. A song-studded romance. Saddle up, you sons of fun. Everybody's flockin' to this one. Curvaceous crusaders battle to rebuild a shattered land. It's love on wheels. The blonde leading the blonde. You'll love every illegal inch of 'em.

They carved a path through the wilderness, and then paved it with bullets, lives, and a romance that rocked the thrones of kings. Heaven could never be this hot and it's all the hell you can handle. Breaking all thrill records. A drama of thundering hoofs and blazing guns through trackless jungles, battling the bloodlust headhunters of the Amazon. Primitive emotions, savage passions, nature in the raw. A frenzied hunt for a hideous beast uncovers an evil cannibal cult and death is the devil's blessing. White heat explodes in the green hell where the dark heart of man comes to burn.

8.

After this week in paradise, they're going to need a vacation of heavy truckin', hard drivin', and free lovin' in South America, where life is cheap. Romantic Rio on a heart-to-heart hook-up with a Greenwich Village cat on the make who ends up with the housewife by mistake. From juke joint to drag strip, it's the livin' end. So much flesh, so little time. Their motive: greed. Their method: murder. Horror and hilarity, mystery and mirth, capering corpses and tangled loves.

Mercenaries of the information, they track the scoop, the death, the madness. It began as a kidnapping. It became a journey of hope. Their rousing story comes roaring across 6,000 miles of excitement. You won't believe your eyes, if you can keep them open. The beaches have become battlefields, the waves are a war zone. A bevy of beauties and a boatload of fun. Each time they kissed there was the thrill of love, the threat of murder. Flaming passions against a background of weird adventure. Six states wanted them jailed. Eight torture victims wanted them dead. All the blood freaks wanted was one more night of the most brutal orgy in history. They're yours, in a heart-walloping love story. See hypnotic love create shocking bestial desire. Women cry for it. Men die for it. The sweet "pill" that makes life bitter. Drug-crazed abandon. Dress sharp. Drive fast. Look cool. Laugh last. Just don't get caught. You've been scared. Now prepare to be terrified. One-way ticket to death. Murder at 90 miles an hour.

Who will survive and what will be left of them? They transplanted a white bigot's head on a soul brother's body. And now with the fights, the fuzz, the chicks, and the choppers, man, they're really in *deeeeep* trouble. He was young, handsome, a millionaire—and he'd just pulled off the perfect crime. She was young, beautiful, a super sleuth—sent to investigate it. Shock-packed story of America's most wanted desperados. Titanic in emotion, in spectacle, in climax. In a jungle war of survival, they learned sacrifice. In a prison of brutal confinement, they found true freedom. A lot of kids get into trouble. These two invented it. Beautiful babes, bashful cowboys. Impassioned by genius. Inflamed by desire. Imprisoned by love. A whole town exploded when a boy and a girl dared go on a journey into love, tears, and laughter on the Sunset Strip, where nothing is deadlier than walking it.

A macabre story of two motorcycle-riding, knife-wielding, shiv-shaving, eye-gouging, arm-twisting, chain-lashing, scalpel-flashing, acid-throwing, gun-shooting, bone-breaking, pathological nuts and their pal the undertaker. Skin diver action, aqualung thrills. They dared enter the cave of death to explore the secrets of hell—an erotic nightmare of tormented lusts that throb in headless, undead bodies. The weird jungle of cobra plants that feed on women and rip men apart. A futuristic subculture erupts from the electronic underground. Desire was their only mistake. Thrill-mad. Without shame. Wanton and dangerous. Whips crack. Swords flash. Bullets fly. A story of casual sins and careless loves. If you're too old, you'll be embarrassed. If you're too young, you won't understand.

9.

America's favorite sweethearts in their final pairing. With Einstein as cupid what could possibly go wrong? Never before were they together again for the second time. The end was just the beginning. There is everything to look forward to, except tomorrow. The story of a night that turned into forever. Blood and guts action from start to finish. It's closer than you think. Earth: it was fun while it lasted. All the time in the world is all they've got. Prepare to fight like there's no tomorrow. Trapped in a world where death is not the end. Houston, we have a problem. Good morning. You are one day closer to the end of the world.

The annihilation of a city is a heartbeat away. Today's terrifying look into what might happen tomorrow. Why are the good people dying? The young and beautiful drained of life? Even the strongest man destroyed by the unholy, even the dead will scream. Fasten your seat belts. You are three-and-a-half blocks away from infinity. Don't kiss me; I'm not dead, yet. The price of admission is the rest of your life. Out of a sea of endless terror, into a world of eternal damnation, it will take you a million light years from home. But will it bring you back? Just when you thought it was safe to die, heaven and earth are about to collide. Full scream ahead. After 5,000 years of civilization, we all need a break. If you have to go to hell, go for a reason. Sooner or later everything goes down. So silent. So deadly. So final.

A world light-years beyond your imagination. Life begins when the world ends. You will orbit into the fantastic future. It's not the end of the world—there's still six hours left.

Helen Does the Hustle

1.

It is true that I have sent six bullets through the head of an old dear friend of mine, Rupert West, tenured professor of Cultural Studies at Miskatonic University and heir apparent to the chair of the humanities department, yet I make this statement in clear and sane mind, to prove, I hope, that I am not his murderer; that some eldritch force butchered his brain long before I did.

Our bosom friendship should not ever have begun, but it did, back in the dawn of the 1990s. That I even finished high school at the time was a miracle, having matriculated at five different institutions in as many different cities, but university beckoned. Miskatonic had recently negotiated a transfer program with the government of Ontario allowing student welfare recipients to continue on assistance after the age of maturity, if they attended the bare minimum of classes—my rotten heart still skips a beat to think of it!

It was through such a program, lubricated as it was with the stardust of humanist thinking, that I found myself at Miskatonic and roommate to Rupert West.

West was a shy, prematurely bald cultural studies major, no happier than when writing about the alienating effects of the disembodied voice of KITT in *Knight Rider* or perusing the rare books collection that Miskatonic was noted for. At any given time, West could be seen struggling across the quad, holding a stack of cursed tomes like *Representing Cthulhu in the Mortal Imagination; Nameless Rites and Wrongs: Problematizing the Endless Void; Everything But the Talent: A Cultural History of Idiot Pan Flute Music; Our Shoggoths, Ourselves;* and *Azathoth and Nyarlathop: The Struggle Against Modernity in the Screaming Abyss.*

Drawn to the rave scene in downtown Arkham, I never studied. While West marked his calendar full of conferences to attend, I lay on our dormitory room floor after imbibing lysergic acid, reading the carpet strands as if they were binary code. "Old boy," West would say to such behavior, "you'll be the death of my concentration." Yet there was a persistent rapport between West and I, tinged with melancholy and what I now know to be the black chords of fate itself. Our friendship only grew as we suffered together through Semiotics 101, taught by that fool hog of a man, Professor Timothy Folliot.

No old curmudgeon, this Folliot was a young, rotund lout who lucked into full tenure after a bungled sexual harassment case found him—unfortunately for decent people everywhere—not guilty. Like an emperor penguin he shuffled around the lecture hall, discouraging discussion, considering the students as no more than writhing krill in his beak while repeatedly mispronouncing the name of the mad Swiss linguist Ferdinand de Saussure. Fed up with being the token impoverished-about-campus and annoyed with the politesse demanded by higher education, I took a paper of mine, some juvenile blather on the resonances between Stonehenge and mall food courts, inserted it into the sleeve of *London Calling* by The Clash, slid it under Folliot's office door, and walked away from Miskatonic forever. Or so I thought.

West continued at Miskatonic through until his graduate years, a task made easier by the sudden disappearance of Professor Folliot. Details were sketchy, but I later heard that Folliot's duplex exploded one night in a spectrum of gassy lights and blood curdling metallic sounds. A graduate student he was secretly living with survived the event, but she was left permanently mad, able only to utter the nonsense words "roh-pah" to attending doctors. She died in the Arkham Center for Mental Health and Outreach several months later, giving birth to a stillborn child, non-human in appearance. Folliot's body was never found.

I drifted through the next decade, ending up—not so strangely given the aimlessness of my pursuits—writing weather copy for an Internet news show that featured nude hosts. I was content to wile my days of sentience away coming up with new single entendres involving the words "hot" and "wet" when an electronic letter from West arrived, bidding with great urgency my return to the hallowed halls of our Miskatonic U. Rah rah rah I remembered chanting at the homecoming games.

2.

The train let me off near the university grounds just before dusk. Making my way to West's office was like falling into a dream of half-remembered corners and dimly lit wheelchair ramps. I found the office and put hand to knob before it struck me. The bastard went and got himself Folliot's former vestibule!

"Davis, old boy!" West exclaimed, pulling the door open and away from me. His voice was strained, and eyes red and puffy, but still he was West, through and through. "Sit down, sit down," he commanded as he led me into the cramped, sepulchral office. "It's been years. Last I heard you were living with a beautician. She wore a space shuttle backpack of some kind as I remember."

"Long gone," I volleyed. "And she was in hairstyling school. But she dropped out because she found the atmosphere too political." West let out a weak chuckle before I continued. "So you have Folliot's office?"

"Man alive, I have his job!" he gloated. "And to a certain extent his legacy."

I looked at the institutional yellow walls, the dying daylight turning the wall burnt umber as we spoke. My eyes darted up to a bookshelf containing multiple copies of West's thesis turned popular syllabus item, *Hulks, Riptides and Magnum PIs: Assaying the Masculine in Reagan-Era Television*. Noticing my lack of enthusiasm, West changed tack: "You never liked Folliot did you? No, I suppose you were too much alike. You could never be told when you were wrong. So you're a writer now?"

"Just for the weather."

"And by what spectral arts do you discern the weather?"

"I rewrite CNN's weather report while imagining someone naked saying it."

West *tsk-tsked* out loud and stood up. "So prosaic a fate, Davis. I thought you would understand what I've been going through. You were, after all, a seeker of arcane knowledge, were you not?"

"What? Because I took you to see *El Topo* once? Out with it, man. Nostalgia was never your strong suit. What's on your mind?"

West walked around his desk with a pedagogic finger pointed at my heart. "Don't you feel it, Davis? Ten years you avoid anything to do with Miskatonic but here you are all of sudden, with one letter from a poor old professor. There's something in you that brought you here tonight."

"Near unemployment?" I offered.

My self-depreciating humor did not dampen West's fervor and I felt a fool for trying to placate him. His eyes, which I'd assumed heavy and red from lack of sleep now took on a singular focus. "Have you heard the larkish formula the physics department is fond of saying about us? That 'Every time someone in the humanities uses the word "quantum," an angel dies'? Well let the angels fall like fruit flies tonight, my friend, because this cultural studies department is onto things the hard sciences are too damned scared to see."

While it is true that the academically inclined are at times barely in touch with us on the other side of the university gates, I knew this to be madness, pure and simple. "What's wrong with two old men in their 30s catching up over dinner at the Insmouth Arms?" I asked in hopes of saving my friend with a little bonhomie. "I remember they had very good calamari."

"It is too late for calamari, Davis! It is a Wednesday-only special."

3.

Though only three hours earlier it had been a warm September day, a chill night now rolled across the campus and West's breath crystallized as he spoke, reminding me on this portentous evening of that constant war of atoms just beyond our vision. "1979 until the end of 1980 were the most calamitous years to ever befall our young democracy, Davis. Pluto moved inside of Neptune's orbit, Three Mile Island, the Sverdlovsk incident, and the final assault on sanity and intellect—"

"Reagan is elected."

"A good student after all, Davis. Overseeing this descent into chaos was an ancient force in the form of electronic transmission. A being so beyond evil, its true, non-Euclidean face would drive any witness mad and—" West interrupted his own deranged sermon. "I can't tell you anymore until we arrive at my house."

We left the campus proper and crossed a street into a neighborhood long favored by faculty. West took us around a corner onto a small street, darker than the rest with streetlamps burnt out and not a single photon of light emitting from any of the dead homes. As we walked closer I noticed each house and apartment block was boarded up, with graffiti taking its rightful, kudzu-like place on every surface. "This exodus," West said while waving his hand around like an ersatz docent, "started after the Folliot Event of 1995. First pets fell ill, then the children. People tried to sell, but then ultimately abandoned their homes. It was Love Canal without a name." We came to an old duplex, all blackened brick and mold-covered siding. West drew close and hissed, his air holding a hint of boozy foulness: "Davis, I am the proud owner of Professor Timothy Folliot's home."

At the entrance West handed me a heavy object wrapped in

oilcloth, telling me to pocket it while he jerked free the rain-swollen door with a pry bar. Once opened, the house seemed to contain a static energy that raised all my hair. "As you can imagine," West continued, "I was the only buyer, though soon after the incident several members of the Aum Shinrikyo death cult were on their way to purchase the house but were turned away at Arkham Airport. A week later they committed their subway attack in Tokyo."

I giggled out loud, which disturbed me so much that I summoned a half explanation: "It's just that the world seems written some days."

"More than you know."

We moved into a scorched living room and West lit a gas lantern, revealing the modernistic sarcophagus in shifting half-light. Co-centric circles etched deep into the wood bare floorboards radiated out from a television set in the corner. "I first came here in a state, the evening after I defended my thesis," West confessed glumly. "I remember getting dressed after the black-robed defense committee bathed me in mead over at Phillips Hall, but nothing more until I found myself standing before the house, the door open. I sat here that night in the most perfect silence I've ever encountered. When I awoke in the morning I wandered to the basement and found this." West produced from his satchel a well-ruffled, Cerloc-bound essay. "*The Ropers: An Ellipsis of Shared Madness* by Timothy Folliot Ph.D." sat in the title cutout window. "I had a piece of the cover analyzed," West spat out. "Human skin."

"Kinko's does interesting work these days, doesn't it?" I quipped.

West admonished me. "This is Folliot's last work! I read it and thought the old man went off the deep end at first. Do you remember the show *The Ropers?*"

"No. But that name. They were the pre–Mr. Furley landlords from *Three's Company?*"

"Yes! Spun off for no particular reason into a new series running from 1979 to 1980. But Folliot dug deeper. Too deep, perhaps." West flipped through the paper and halted at an image of twin horned and winged figures. "It's a kind of statue that dates from Sumeria, 30th century BC. The figures are found throughout the era, often just outside of dwelling sites. Archeologists thought at first they were protective figures, but a tablet discovered just 20 years ago states otherwise. They're demons, going by the shared name, Ro-Pa, and were meant as vassals, heralding the coming of those who cannot be named."

"You're as mad as Folliot! Norman Fell, a Sumerian demon?" I felt queer, and my feet weakened in that stygian blackness.

"No, fool. Norman Fell was just another pawn in a grand work that Folliot was only beginning to figure out before his death. Ro-Pa next emerge in Turkey in the middle ages and from there, the legend travels to Central Europe where Ro-Pa become the Ropers of peasant folklore. They're innkeepers whose home was the gateway to Hell for unwary travelers, unless the travelers appeased the Ropers by leaving their shoes filled with marzipan outside their bedroom door—still a tradition to this day in Bulgaria. And then nothing until the late 1970s. Some folklorists at the time of *Three's Company* noted the coincidence of the Roper name and occupation with the myth, and the show *was* banned in Bulgaria, but it wasn't until *The Ropers* premiered that very disturbing things began happening. With every airing of every episode of *The Ropers* the average amount of ambient radiation nationwide increased 400 per cent for a period of 30 minutes. These effects also correlated with the increase of Reagan's popularity in the polls—*to the decimal point!*"

Playing along with West, I said, "Perhaps. But the show ended and the world didn't."

"I cannot answer you. Something stopped it. The show was canceled. Reagan was weakened by the assassination attempt. And most people cannot remember the show. Whatever force it was, it retreated into the unconscious murk, until Folliot called it forth again. He searched for tapes. Nothing. No bootlegs. He could only study the show plots by interviewing imprisoned pedophiles and Republican speechwriters. They are the only two populations who remember watching it. The ABC archives hung up on Folliot when he phoned. Most of the cast had committed suicide or died of strange cancers."

West walked over to the TV set and switched it and an old VCR on, filling the air with the scent of burnt dust. "Funny," West said with bemusement. "There's no power on the entire block, but this works."

I shoved my cold hands into my jacket pockets and dislodged from its wrapping the object West had given me. It was a pistol. I grasped it in my pocket while West descended further into lunacy.

"The day he died, Folliot received a tape in the mail of the final unaired episode of *The Ropers*. Today, I received my own copy, just before you arrived. My own reward for taking cultural studies too far." West took a videocassette out of his satchel and snapped open its malodorous black plastic case. "The episode is titled, 'Helen Does the Hustle' and I rather prefer that you shoot me before I press play. I know I can't stop myself."

"Wait!" I cried.

West inserted the tape and pressed play and I was thrown to the ground by an energy wave, my eardrums instantly burst and bleeding from a high frequency noise. I struggled up upon my feet again. The TV screen screamed static and tendrils of rotten light emerged and embraced West, seeping under his skin and turning his eyes glassy and black—a blind idiot god! His head lolled back in my direction.

The dread thing that was once Rupert West smiled and opened its mouth, hissing in a glass shard voice, "I did it for the Gipper."

I shot all the bullets, deregulating him, as you might say. The TV turned off of its own accord, its signal retreating down to a slowly fading white dot while the soulless West-thing let go of its final sulfurous exhalations.

4.

The ten years between now and my term at Miskatonic were lost ones, and in the last few months before I came back I often woke up in the middle of the night mourning for that dead time. But I have now found a purpose I can be proud of, always a difficult achievement for a non-college graduate.

I and what's left of West are still here in the former home of Timothy Folliot, Ph.D. The videocassette is still sitting in that old belt-driven contraption. I've attempted to smash the infernal machine several ways with various objects but it will not break, and with each impotent strike the damn thing only rings back with the pure tone of a tuning fork.

So "Helen Does the Hustle" and I remain here, perhaps forever, or at least until my death, and I am content and fulfilled, guarding the abomination until that time, keeping the gibbering chaos of 1980 from ever returning.

But the days here in this cursed duplex are long, and every now and then I catch myself drifting away, chanting out loud, "Ro-Pa, Ro-Pa, Ro-Pa . . ."

The Unicorns, Part Two

expir: 26/feb/2016

January 09, 2018 07:03

39065109091221
Ronald   30/Jan/2018
Reagan, my father :
[stories] (CheckOut)

Total   1 Item(s)

When the man and woman asked if they could check their e-mail on your computer you were tired of writing anyway. Writing wasn't so strange, after all. You had been raised in a light industry household, and ever since you could stand you had been stuffing into cardboard envelopes recordings of songs about Watergate set to unsure waltzes. You're used to repeating action until you forget what you're doing. Writing had a hidden rhythm, too.

Sitting down was different, though. Writing was as much like not-working as it was like working. As dead spots of numbness spread across your thighs and your hip joints, you noticed your captors changing. The man's eyes drifted and he did not move. The woman who had demanded to be called Shadowfax was fidgety, picking at her ear and adjusting her Bedazzled jean jacket. You decided these were their true faces, how fate had decreed they appear throughout the days when they weren't waving guns around. Just as the rest of life had bored your captors, you had bored them as well.

The checking of e-mail begat the checking of Facebook, through which they followed several links and wound up in a debate among fantasy horse-character afficionados.

"You don't have Skype on this?" the man asked, more wounded than angry.

That was hours ago, and you even dozed off for a little while sitting on the floor. You got up and thought of telling them you were going to the can, but they, too, had found the rhythms of typing and staring, and had forgotten you.

Walking into the back of the shop and out the door was so easy you paused and contemplated its narrative soundness. *Is that something writers do every day?* you asked yourself.

You wanted to experiment with the truth. You wrote in your mind: *The unicorn is unemployed.*

With that one line, would a reader imagine a unicorn on a couch surrounded by an empty six-pack of Pabst, sighing, "Just my luck, I guess," while attempting to work the remote with his hooves?

Why did "the unicorn" work better than "my father"? Fiction made things better, you realized, and people sure liked unicorns better than people.

Despite your exhaustion, you had to run back into your office to write it down before you forgot, and maybe even ask the man and woman if they could believe in a unicorn drinking beer in sunlit tedium, cursing your name, and the obsolescence you had written him into.

Notes and Acknowledgments

"Ordinary People" first appeared on *Joyland*.

"Johnny" was created by collecting Johnny-dialogue from over two years of film watching. A performance of it was presented by the Mercer Union Center for Contemporary Art in 2009. The compete text was published in *Drunken Boat*.

"The Libertine" first appeared in *Matrix*.

"Bury My Heart at Tataouine" first appeared on *The Fanzine*.

"The Lame Shall Enter at Five Miles Per Hour" first appeared on *CellStories*.

"Voice Over" was created by sorting through 5,000 different film taglines. A shorter version was performed by a voice over artist for a gallery project. This complete version of the script was first published on Ubu.com and in the anthology *Against Expression* (Northwestern University Press).

Thank you: Michael Holmes and everyone at ECW Press, *Matrix*, Mercer Union, Kenneth Goldsmith and Ubu.com, *The Fanzine*, Dan Sinker and *CellStories*, Sina Queyras and *Drunken Boat*, and everyone at *Joyland*.

Thanks to all the performers who helped adapt these works.

Thank you Faye Guenther and Jenny Sampirisi for being an editorial and marketing focus group of educated women aged 25 to 35 currently earning median incomes.

This book is for my wife, Emily Schultz.

About the Author

Brian Joseph Davis is an artist and the author of *Portable Altamont,* a collection that garnered praise from *Spin* magazine for its "elegant, wise-ass rush of truth, hiding riotous social commentary in slanderous jokes." *Slate* called *I, Tania,* his first novel, "the book of your fever dreams." His media art has been acclaimed by *Wired, Pitchfork, Salon,* and *LA Weekly,* which wrote, "Davis has an amazing head for aural experiments that are smart on paper and fascinating in execution."

Davis is co-founder of Joyland.ca, which the CBC called "the go-to spot for readers seeking the best in short fiction."